A
LEAP
OF
EVOLUTION

They weren't giant monsters or creatures from outer space. They were just ants. No bigger than a fingernail.

So why couldn't anyone stop them?

An astonishing leap of evolution had given birth to a new insect race, more intelligent and civilized than any other creature on earth—including Man. They knew how to adapt to poisons, how to defend themselves against the mightiest weapons men could devise.

And now they would dictate surrender terms to the human race....

D0668651

PHASE IV
is an original POCKET BOOK edition.

Books by Barry N. Malzberg

Beyond Apollo
Destruction of the Temple
Phase IV

Published by POCKET BOOKS

PHASE IV

by
Barry N. Malzberg

PUBLISHED BY POCKET BOOKS NEW YORK

PHASE IV

POCKET BOOK edition published November, 1973
5th printing.........................July, 1974

Σ

This original POCKET BOOK edition is printed from brand-new plates made from newly set, clear, easy-to-read type. POCKET BOOK editions are published by POCKET BOOKS, a division of Simon & Schuster, Inc., 630 Fifth Avenue, New York, N.Y. 10020. Trademarks registered in the United States and other countries.

Standard Book Number: 671-77710-6.

Cover photograph by Dr. H. S. Banton.
Printed in the U.S.A.

This one is for Bob Gleason.

PHASE I

Time: Something clicked and in the nebula shaped like a spirochete, a bolt of energy moved from one side to the other, seventeen light-years, and then vaulted into pure space. Pure space was another two hundred thousand light-years, and the energy, now compacted, whisked through it like a fish through water, accelerating, the inside curiously static.

Time: Something attacked the energy, some cosmic turbulence or another intelligence, impossible to tell, and the energy felt itself being squeezed, became sentient then, and fought back. Somewhere in the Crab cluster, the attacker and the intelligence fought, and the battle lasted for fifteen thousand years. Then the attacker fell away like ash and the energy continued on its journey. Intelligence withdrew. At some subliminal level it meditated.

The system rotated around a small Class B star, the star almost a dwarf, in a far sector of the Milky Way. The sun in normal cycle would approach nova in fifteen billion years, burn out then and consume the system. Now it was still on the upswing. The radiance from this star drew the approaching energy to life once again and it became sensate. It probed through channels of recollection in a way that both was and was not conscious.

It landed on the third planet.

Although the energy, long compressed for the journey, was only the size of a small stone now, three inches across, six inches wide and deep, the impact tore at it as it skittered through the sands, and for a long, long time it existed in a state of nonconsciousness. At some base level, it struggled for survival, to combat the injury of the impact, and it did not seem that it would survive, but the traveler was strong—its makers had prepared it for this—and after an inconceivably long time, it began to gather strength once again. It had passed the point of survival. Moistened by rain, sheltered by the sands, the energy slowly returned to its full awareness, and then it broke free of the stone, probing with fine tentacles of consciousness for contact.

Contact: It found the minds that it was seeking. The minds were vegetative, possessed intelligence unlike any conventional notions of reason . . . but they were linked in a clear dependency, a fine network of connection spreading from one mind to the next, and in the midst of those connections the stone sent, for the second time in its journey, a bolt of energy, much weaker, but sufficient to do the necessary. Under the thrust of that bolt, the minds quickened. Something

8

happened to them, the connections became broader, richer, deeper in stroke. They keened to one another. Connection became a fine mesh.

Now under the guidance of the stone, the quickened intelligences were working. From various parts there was a gathering: instructions were passed and with precision the next part of the project, one that could only be accomplished through directed effort, was started. The minds scurried. The stone beneath them extended visual centers to see what was happening, and all was going as it should and it felt pleasure. Available to it was a welter of emotions, but it discarded all but the pleasure, worked upon it, then sent it on a narrow thread to those it controlled. They throbbed with gratification.

The slabs grew. Seven of them on the desert, white, six feet in height, cunningly hollowed out, where at the stone's orders, their horrid secrets began to pulsate. Complex readjustments were made in the biological system of the intelligences; from those changes came something that both was and was not like them. One within a slab, guarded from the landscape, those things grew.

At length, the stone on the desert felt the vast weakness that comes when a task is completed, knowing this without questioning. Although it was very complex and subtle, it was ultimately only a tool, and when a tool's work is done, it must be put away. Without remorse, regret, or a sense of loss, the thing encapsulated in the stone considered the fact of its death and then, almost casually, shut down certain intricate facets. The energy within it flickered, flamed, and perished.

The thing died and at the instant of its death, a hundred million light-years away, in a checking-center that had been waiting since the journey began, a message was received. OPERATIVE the message said, although in no language that could be understood, for it was a language not composed of sound but of light and distance.

Inside the towers, things grew.

II

The ants were breeding now, and what came out of the queens in the slabs were ants of a different sort, inheriting the new method of connection. The older ants, some of them, clung tenaciously to their own habits, but the life cycles of ants are quite short, and those that emerged from the queens were strong. The larvae burst from the eggs, rested awhile, and then foraged out into the desert on their complex but ultimately simple task.

An old worker ant, stumbling through one of the slabs, passed into the queen's belly and attempted to rupture it. The queen screamed without sound and in a few seconds there were one hundred, two hundred soldiers that entered the slab and tore the worker ant apart before it had time to flee. But the martyrdom of the worker seemed to inspire a horde of other workers, the older ones, the ones who had been there before something (which their intelligences could only understand as an intrusion) had happened, and they fought fiercely, desperately, the green and red of their bodies locked into the black and white streaked forms of the new soldiers. The battle went on inside the slab under the strange, hollow eyes of the great queen, five feet high, who watched implacably from a hundred pinpoints of light, and for a while it seemed that the older workers might actually win because they were fighting with the inheritance of a hundred million years of knowledge. For them and their ancestors it had always been this way, and their cilia and mouths stroked out vicious patterns . . . but the battle turned, it would have to turn, the soldiers were faster and cleverer than the older workers, and they had, under the eyes of the great queen, a seeming contempt toward death that the workers simply could not match. Five hundred, a thousand of the black and white ants fell, but more were spewed forth into the slab, the unmoving queen watching, and soon enough the older workers began to fall, first in hundreds and then thousands, red and green bodies covering the bottom of the slab like ash, spilling out into the desert, their juices mingling into and spotting the sands and—

—The soldiers carried their dead out of the slab and buried them with the corpses of the enemy and in the other five slabs the same thing, at intervals, was happening.

Soon there were very few red and green ants left, and those that were had merely inherited pigmentation.

All of this took about six years that, to the queens, were negligible. Time was no factor. No one noticed the slabs.

III

The rabbit sprang from a clump of bushes, seeing something that its brain registered as terrible danger, then attempted to break free and run the length of the strip, past the slabs, into a clump of mesquite that looked safe. Ants appeared in its path, leapt upon it, but the rabbit brushed them off, one foot, then the other clearing its hindquarters, throwing off the bodies of the ants, spewing them from its mouth. The ants were small, and although the rabbit was possessed with fear, it did not seem that they posed any danger; but they kept on coming, emerging from the sands to seize the rabbit's throat, some of them getting into the corners of its eyes. Blinded, the rabbit rolled on the sands to free itself, but everywhere it rolled there were ants, they came into its ears, anus, nostrils, clambering within. The rabbit continued to twist on the sands, but a hundred ants raced through the snug caverns inside the rabbit's body, biting, severing, tormenting . . . the spinal cord was severed with a thousand bites, and the rabbit lay paralyzed on the desert floor. Unblinking, its distended eyes looked up at the sun exploding before it.

The ants fed.

There was no wastage. They were very hungry, but the choicest parts were taken back to the queens.

IV

Ants now teemed through that area of the Arizona desert, working out from the slabs in a fine spidery network. They were very busy and they needed no rest. Their life cycles were only a month, but the queens thriving on their diet, were spewing out a million a day now, and each of the ants was as careless of its survival as were the queens. There was no such thing as death for any of the ants because the intelligences resided in the slabs. The ants were merely extensions. They worked like fingers on the desert: patting, arranging, spreading. Occasionally they talked to one another without language. They gave one another commands.

Some kind of poisonous spray was thrown over them and several million died before the queens were able to breed immunology. These newer ants and the survivors who had been originally immune buried their dead.

V

The slabs, parched by sun, now rose higher, ten feet or more, giving room for the expanding queens. The sun had bleached them free of color, and they stood gray against the desert, reaching.

VI

The queens felt imminence and made certain adjustments. All thus far had been preparation; now, inevitably, that time of preparation was done. The enemy, heightened to awareness, was coming.

The queens sent out signals to the workers, who withdrew to safe positions. They waited.

The queens in their slabs mused.

PHASE II

Lesko's Diary: Hubbs says that this is a relatively simple assignment; that some rearrangement in the ecosystem will have to be made and should not take us more than two weeks to find the problem and set the balance again, but I am not so sure of this. I do not like the situation.

Hubbs has been involved in pure research for too long; he is demoniac, possessed, at least this is my guess. He has manipulated abstractions for so long that it is as if personality has fallen away from the man —a thin, balding, obsessed fifty-year-old individual. He approaches what may be an ecological disaster as a simple problem in applied ecology and has to be a little mad. Of course it is possible that he is not at all mad and that I am overreacting. I have been on the pure research bit somewhat too long myself, and there is something about the behavior pattern of whales observed up close for eight months that could unstring a man of somewhat simpler psychological makeup than myself. Whales are so *ponderous*. What I need is a long rest, but I do not think that this expedition into the Arizona desert is quite the ticket.

Hubbs does. Hubbs's optimism may be psychopathic, but it has the convincing nature of psychopathology. "Isn't that interesting?" he said when he informed me back in San Francisco that I had been drafted as his assistant by the National Science Foundation . . . at his request. Ants being more viable than whales, I suppose.

"What we've seen in that desert in the last few months appears to be a complete breakdown of normal ecological checks and balances. The ants are multiplying like crazy out there because something is checking their natural enemies: mantises, spiders, gophers, coyotes. It must be a very strong breed of ants, eh Lesko? Eh?"

His eyes twinkled and this must have been the first time that it occurred to me he was mad. "Great panic, Lesko!" he went on. "Residents fleeing, homesteads abandoned, that entire patch of desert being left to an uncontrollable onslaught of ants! Like a science-fiction movie, wouldn't you say? The ants are taking over! The invasion of the ant-people! Well," he said, returning to a somewhat more level tone of voice, "we'll go out there and take a look at this. We've got a station, computer, equipment, and a great deal of insecticide. All in all, I think that we'll take care of this invasion of the ant-people in two or three weeks, Lesko, and then you can return to your whales. You'll appreciate the break from routine."

I am not sure. I am just not so sure of this. Perhaps

16

it is merely atavism, that ancient quality lurking in the back of all our minds—primitive dread, superstition, the Jungian subconscious I believe they call it— but the specter of ants taking over a section of the Arizona desert, driving people from their homes, apparently suspending all ecological data . . . this inspires dreams and intimations that I find quite difficult to handle, and recent nights have been long, parched exercises in nightmare. Of all the intelligences on this planet, of course, those of the ants are most foreign to us, and for that reason the most menacing . . . they simply do not think or behave as all other creatures do but on some level that our best researches can hardly verbalize. They are particles of subliminal intelligence, I suppose, incredibly earnest, very organized, always busy . . . and they are the only survivors (always excepting the roaches, which are an urban problem) from the Cretaceous age, and that must tell us something. Dinosaurs, stegosauri, Neanderthals, mammoths, saber-toothed tigers, to say nothing of the geography of the poles themselves . . . all gone for millions of years. Yet the ants survive in almost the exact form that they had then. Should this teach us something? Yes, gentlemen, it should teach us something.

Hubbs laughs and says that there was always a fear of the ants taking over, and here, perhaps, in an obscure portion of the Southwest the little buggers are at last getting to the job. His laughter to me is insanity, because if this is true, and I do not think that Hubbs realizes this, we are all in very serious trouble. The entire network of man's living pattern—speaking ecologically—is one that has gone in the opposite direction of ant intelligence and has now reached a great level of intricacy, verbalization, abstraction, interdepend-

ence. The ant intelligence, which is highly coopera-
tive, entirely subvocal, and extremely organized
could be malignant to us . . . if for some reason
that intelligence turned against us.

Enough of this anxiety neurosis; it comes from being
thirty-five years old, unmarried, too deep into abstraction myself, working too hard, thinking too much,
needing a long rest. Needing a good woman. It may
be that I see Hubbs so clearly and distrust him because
he is a projection of myself as I may be in twenty
years: pure, neurotic intelligence incapable of feeling,
no grasp of metaphor. I have been too long with my
whales. I should have gotten married years ago, but
who, who, who would have me?

I am frightened.

II

"The evidence at hand," Hubbs said, bouncing
along in the Willys jeep, Lesko struggling with the
wheel, trying to keep the overloaded vehicle straight
on the negligible desert highway, "is a sudden and
dramatic disappearance of several species of preda-
tor insect . . . principally mantises, beetles, millipedes,
and spiders."

"That's right," Lesko said. He wiped the sweat from
his forehead. "That much was made clear from the beginning."

"Don't interrupt me," Hubbs said. "I want to lay

this out for you very carefully. The hypothesis to be confirmed is an equally dramatic increase in the population of insects normally controlled by these predators. I refer to ants."

"Right," Lesko said.

The sun was pitiless. It would be good to get into the fully air-conditioned and insulated station, but the only way to get there was to track through this hell. Lesko squinted, put both hands on the wheel, and maneuvered the jeep painfully around a small open hole in the roadway.

"Thirdly," Hubbs said, "proposal." He took off his glasses, rimmed sweat from his eyes, replaced his glasses, and then went on. "We will see the effects of a biological imbalance on life forms in the subject area . . . with the emphasis on population dynamics, density controls, species diversity, dominance hierarchies. And genetic aberrations, if any."

"Of course," Lesko said, looking back.

"Mode of operation, number four," Hubbs said. Lesko looked at him sidewise and saw for the first time that Hubbs had not been speaking extemporaneously; he was reading from a sheet of paper that he held before him, covered with painful cursive symbols. "An experimental station to be located, built, and maintained with appropriate equipment for the study and analysis of the ant population." He put the paper beside him with a flourish. "That station is already available," he said.

"Yes," Lesko said. "I know." The jeep now took them by an abandoned field to their right, in front of which a sign COUNTRY CLUB hung supported by wire. Four weeks ago there had been people here, people on the golf course beyond it; now all of them were gone, the population cleared out. Hubbs and he were probably the only human beings within an area of ten square miles, and this made him shudder, just the two of them and the mysterious ants ... but Hubbs seemed quite pleased with the idea. The thing about Hubbs was that he probably would have been happiest of all with no company, but the Coronado Institute, under whose auspices this had been financed, was a little bit stuffy about sending out one man. They had wanted four or five for simple backup and checking procedures if nothing else. But Hubbs had managed to persuade them to settle for one. Lesko. That he had been specifically requested was supposed to be an honor. *Honor.* Why did I take it? Lesko thought, not for the first or tenth time, what persuaded me to get into this? He had no answer. There was some question of compulsion here.

"Personnel," Hubbs was saying, looking at his sheet of paper again. "One senior scientist—myself that is —plus one associate to be named. Now named. James R. Lesko. Temporary personnel for construction and installation as noted in the budget."

Lesko passed a sign that said PARADISE CITY in clumsily painted letters, and then, that quickly, they were in the middle of what had been a development in the process of completion. Half-completed houses, half-filled roadways, foundations. A few television antennaes coming forlornly from a few of the houses that had been completed. Open storefronts, some of them with signs half-painted. Lesko felt the revulsion beginning again—it was such a human thing, this abandoned Paradise City, and yet it had been rendered inhuman. He slowed the jeep, picking out a point of orientation. The station would be somewhere on the outskirts, toward the west, he thought. Where was the west? Sweeping the landscape he saw nothing. "Keep on going," Hubbs said. "It's set low to the ground." Not reading from the paper his voice was high, less certain. "Concentrate on your driving, don't look at things."

"All right," Lesko said. "All right." He accelerated fiercely, the jeep holding low to the ground, and they drove through Paradise City at forty or fifty miles an hour, bouncing and jouncing on the seats, possessions behind them sliding but prevented by the lash rope from dropping to the baking road surface. "Where are these so-called towers?"

"Towers?" Hubbs said absently. "Oh, yes, towers. We'll see them later." His voice changed; he started to read again. "Supplementary request," he said. "In the light of certain events reported in the subject area, and my monograph in this regard may take reference, certain additional funds are requested from the director's discretionary budget, plus the services of a qualified information specialist with a cryptological background. In this connection," Hubbs said, Lesko yanking the jeep down a long, empty street of ruined and empty buildings that opened on a long view of the desert, now choked with haze, "I have been most impressed with the recent work of James R. Lesko . . . at the Naval Undersea Center at San Diego, and I am requesting his assignment as my associate for a period of time not to exceed twenty-one days." He put the papers away and for the first time smiled. "End of memo," he said.

"I don't think it will be twenty-one days," Lesko said.

"It probably won't be. It should as a matter of fact be a great deal less." Hubbs leaned over, seeing something through the windshield. "There," he said. "I believe we have found our victim."

Lesko followed the man's pointing finger and saw

the towers. They were just beyond what probably would have been the far edge of the development, seven slabs eight to ten feet high, clearly visible now as the jeep bore down on them. Even as he looked at them, he felt an oddly disconcerted feeling as if some power, some quality of noise were emanating . . . but this at least he put down to nervous exhaustion. The slabs were merely that, pieces of concrete, nothing more. Until recently they had attracted so little attention that it had been possible for the builders to complete half of the development without really noticing them. They must have taken them for artifacts . . . indeed, Lesko thought rather wryly, the slabs might have struck them as being a possible selling point. *Natural stone wonders,* or whatever. The imaginations of the developers were inexhaustible that way . . . until and unless, of course, they ran out of money.

"End of the line," Hubbs said briskly. "Let's have a close look at them."

Lesko found himself in a shallow field. He bumped the jeep to a point about ten feet downrange from the slabs, put the emergency brake on, and shut off the engine. Insects battered the windshield, swooped around them. Otherwise it was quiet. Lesko could see no sign of ants. Maybe it was a rumor. Panic. Hysteria. A sudden unexplained increase in the ant population, one of those things that could happen in a desert already eaten away by an ecological righting. He shook his head and clambered heavily out of the vehicle. Hubbs was already near the slabs, kneeling, inspecting them with enthusiasm.

"Remarkable," Hubbs said as Lesko came up to him. "Probably there is some direct connection here with the ant population. Eventually we'll have to take them apart of course." He stood slowly and looked up the impassive face of the nearest slab, hands on hips. "No indication of origin," he said. "Artifacts, of course, but of what?"

Lesko walked past the line of slabs. He had a sudden and total lack of interest in them. It was mysterious; they had traveled a hundred miles to see them, and yet here at last, he wanted only to get away. Was it possible that they were emanating a wave that made him feel this way? Ridiculous . . . and yet dolphins had sonar. He looked at a collapsed house some distance away, the last outpost of the ruined development. It looked as if it had been imploded, cheap furniture, plaster, glass lay together unevenly on a foundation. It was a picture of complete disaster; yet it did not seem to concern Hubbs at all. Hubbs's eyes were bright as he looked at the fallen timbers, then back to the slabs.

"No bodies . . . I hope," Lesko said.

"The population evacuated themselves some days ago."

Lesko and Hubbs walked to the foundation. Probably this house had been intended to be the showpiece of the development: *Wake up every morning in the shadow of mysterious, ten-foot artifacts.* Yes, that would be how they would have promoted it. There were people who liked that kind of thing. You just could not comprehend fully the perversity of humanity, its endless variety, the range of behavior. "You have some powerful friends," he said to Hubbs, looking at the walls.

"Wind and weather did most of it, I would say. Call it just another desert development that didn't develop."

"And then the ants finished it off?"

23

"We'll have to find out about that," Hubbs said. "I would say that there was more panic in the flight of the residents than actual, ah, menace presented by the ants. The landscape would contribute to it, of course." He shrugged. "This couldn't have been a very tasteful environment, Paradise City."

"I don't know," Lesko said. "This house hasn't simply fallen away. It's been *attacked*."

"Um," Hubbs said and took out a small camera to almost absently shoot a couple of standing pictures of the house. "Mr. Lesko, you did your major work in applying game theory to the language of killer whales, is that correct?"

"Well," Lesko said, "it proved to be cheaper than applying it to roulette."

"Did you actually make any positive contact with the whales?" Hubbs said, toying with the camera, then replacing it. "Or was it—"

"Only with the emotionally disturbed."

"Oh?" Hubbs said. "How were you able to determine the emotional disturbance?"

"We talked about it a bit. They opened their hearts to me."

Hubbs's features broke open into an uneasy smile. "I assume you're joking," he said.

Lesko felt a flush building around his cheeks. Hubbs was a small man, not only physically but at a certain level of emotional vulnerability. It was not so much, he saw, that Hubbs was possessed by abstraction as that almost everything else frightened him. He did not know the language of contact . . . but this was as much Lesko's fault because he was only one of a number of people who had never tried to teach him.

"I'm sorry," he said. "I'm just a pencil and paper

guy. I wouldn't know the front end of a whale from a . . . well, from a hole in the ground."

Hubbs turned and walked the other way, picking his way through the ruined foundation. Lesko followed him, staring at the towers. There seemed to be a certain *light*—

"I know that games are your business, James," Hubbs said uncomfortably. "You play them well and that's why you're here. We're going to apply game theory to see if we can establish some kind of communication. But this is a very serious business."

"Isn't that the best kind?" Lesko said, fascinated by the towers. He could not decide exactly what the material was; it was, he suspected, of a chemical compound that no one on earth could fabricate. It was dirt, a kind of closely packed silt, irregular up and down the columns, but the design, he thought, had an odd rigidity, the angles were sculptured, coming together at certain points in an odd and precise honeycomb. And now that he looked through the dazzle of the sun, was it possible that the towers seemed to have *faces*—

Suddenly he wanted to look at them no more. Hubbs had gone ahead. Lesko scurried to keep up with him.

III

Lesko's Diary: But it turns out that there are a few people here—besides Hubbs and myself that is to say—and one of them, no less, is an attractive girl. It would be nice to think that this is a sign that things are looking up, but I do not think that they are looking up at all; rather, the fact that there are people holding out on this terrain has somehow raised the stakes. It is not just Hubbs and myself now. It is not a mere research project. There is, so to speak, a human element, and meanwhile things are moving so rapidly already that I fear they may be out of control.

After we left the towers, getting back into the jeep, I felt somewhat better. It is hard to express exactly what power they exert upon me, but there is a kind of profound unease here, something perhaps better unphrased here in what I originally intended to be a scientific journal chock-full of routine observations on the progress of the project. Sufficient to say that I do not think that those towers were made by anything human, but I do not, then, know what made them nor do I want to find out. Moving away from them in the jeep I felt better, better yet because of my insight into Hubbs. I could work with this man now because I thought I understood him. Similarly with whales.

Driving toward the station a few miles from the towers, we saw airborne helicopters dangling cargo supplies. They flew low and men stretched out to wave their hands at us. The hardware was coming. Computer, provisions, insulation, wiring . . . the station would be converted into an impregnable, functioning, and military base within twenty-four hours, and this made me feel almost cheerful. My mood of depression seemed to lift in the singing and clattering of the engines, and I said to Hubbs, "If the people around here ran away because they saw what the ants were doing . . . then I wonder what the ants will do when they see what *we're* doing." And this was a cheerful thought; how could these creatures, even assuming a malevolence that we had no right whatsoever to assume, stand up against ordnance. Certainly there were a *lot* of them . . . but we had the firepower if necessary to annihilate every ant in the world. The only reason that they had survived from Cretaceous times is that they had posed no threat to man; if they had, they would have gone the way of the mammoth or for that matter the Neanderthal (that threatening subhuman presence that Cro-Magnon could not abide) and just be sure of that.

"Perhaps they'll laugh," Hubbs said with that strange seriousness of his.

I said, "That would show no sensitivity whatsoever," and Hubbs grinned at that, the first time I had gotten through, by God. Then just as I thought that I had the situation under control and understood at last, Hubbs was staring out the jeep at what appeared to be clouds in the distance and said, "You know, there *is* someone still around here. Doesn't that look like a tractor?"

Yes, it did look like a tractor. We drove toward a patch of desert where clouds of dust were being moved around by an elderly man in a large orange vehicle, pipe in his mouth, working on the patch of dirt with the maniacal singlemindedness of a Man Who Believes He Can Make A Difference, puffing foul clouds of smoke into the air from a pipe, humming to himself above the whine of machinery, so absorbed in his task that Hubbs had to lean on the horn with growing fury to finally attract his attention. Slowly, the man acknowledged us, took off his hat, waved, cut the machine with the aspect of a man who is living in a different kind of time, where chronology means nothing and only the instant moment counts, walked over to the tractor base, checked it out, then came to us nodding. Hubbs asked what the hell he was doing here, a reasonable question, although, of course, the man was not doing anything illegal. (Hubbs has a passionate sense of order; if he hears that a place is abandoned, then by God it ought to be abandoned.) The man said that he was digging a ditch and then motioned back in the distance where we could see a farmhouse, little curls of smoke coming from this pastoral refuge, "Name's Clete," he said like a character in some half-forgotten rustic play. "I work for Eldridge over there. Come on," he said, "you want to see Eldridge?"

I guess we did. Eldridge seemed to be worth seeing; if ever a man believed that life must go on and be damned if he would be driven from routine, it would have to be this one. Clete motioned us out of the jeep and led us down rows and rows of plants toward the farmhouse. In a ravine on the way, we saw a dead sheep lying amidst vegetation. Clete paused, said he wanted to show us something, and then, going to the sheep, exposed the neck through the folds and showed us the four small holes there. He did this in a horrid, matter-of-fact way, and I thought I would retch, but Hubbs was fascinated. He forgot, almost at once, that the presence of Clete or Eldridge was somehow a personal attack upon the project and joined Clete at the animal, stroking away at the neck folds. "Remarkable," he said when they had returned and we had continued toward the farmhouse. "There are several African ants that will attack anything . . . insect, animal, anything at all that threatens their food supply. The smell triggers the behavior." He continued chattering to me as we walked on, Clete leading and poking through the vegetation. I failed to detect any more sheep corpses, which disconcerted me not a bit.

The farmhouse itself was another ruined, rotted structure, but it was a human ruination, if it is clear what I am saying; Eldridge lived in dishevelment obviously because he was comfortable that way, and the farmhouse in its noisome deterioration was probably contrived as carefully for that effect as the ragged clothes of rich young people. Eldridge, a calm, sturdy man in his sixties, another pipe smoker, nodded at us as if he had been expecting a visit for a long time, almost as if we were there to give him approval and assistance, and took us around the house, showing the system of shallow ditches in which pipe had been laid, probably by Clete. He had been digging a ditch farther out when we found him. Eldridge pointed from the pipes to a large oil tank behind the house, and his face was suffused with pleasure. He did not seem to mind the ants; he took them as a challenge. "This here," he said, "this is what we're doing. We're running lines from the fuel tank, you understand, and if those ants get over the water trap, why then we're going to set fire to this ditch and watch them all die." He smiled. "I'm looking forward to that," he said. "The filthy little buggers aren't going to take my land from me. The fact is," he went on, "I'm almost enjoying this. I'm going to survive and be the better for it." Leaning on a hoe he looked like something out of *American Gothic*, although, perhaps, less pessimistic. "Don't you think I've done a good job?" he said.

"I think you've done very well indeed," Hubbs said, and a look passed between them, call it communion or mutual respect, but it was apparent that Eldridge was doing exactly what Hubbs imagined he would do in this circumstance; he was Taking A Stand, he was Not Being Intimidated. It affected me

29

to see Hubbs responding in this way, and I realized that he was glad to see that Eldridge had held out. The abandoned Paradise City must have affected him as deeply as me in a different way. Suddenly I liked Hubbs much more.

Eldridge suggested that we might as well sit and stay for a while, and that seemed all right to me, all right to Hubbs as well. Clete went and got some chairs and we all went to the porch a-setting and a-rocking, meeting Eldridge's wife, Mildred, a grim, determined woman with the same hardness that Eldridge had, but with something softer behind the eyes that indicated that she could both participate in defiance with him and not take it that seriously. And we met Eldridge's granddaughter, Kendra.

Well, music and bells for the others, please; I am not a sentimental man. I will admit that Kendra has already had a great affect on me, but I try not to take this kind of thing too seriously. She is an attractive girl in her late teens; all right, she is *more* than attractive, a softness and grace is there that lifts her entirely out of the context of mere prettiness and touches me deeply.

My relationships with women, fragmentary at best, have not been so good since I got into whale research (something that this journal already has made clear, I suspect); but I do not think, never thought, that this was so much my fault as the fault of the women themselves. There are very few I have met through the years who struck me as being worth the effort . . . and for me at least a below-standard woman simply poses no interest at all. Perhaps this makes me a very strange man, but I have never been overly concerned with the fact that most of the time my sexual drive seems to flicker away at a subliminal level, only making its presence known at rare occasions and then always with women like Kendra to whom sexual interest is merely a confirmation of feelings they have already aroused. I realize that I am becoming somewhat confused about this and giving more attention to my feelings than they are really worth, but I want to get this absolutely straight, and if this journal is going to stand up as being of any scientific validity—which I trust it will—then it is not a negligible part of the scientific method that the prejudices and nature of the writer be themselves revealed, integrated as it were into the core of the work. She is a beautiful girl; at another time, in another way, something might have happened here, but I am too preoccupied with the ants. And as Hubbs has made clear over and again this is no pleasure trip. I have been with my whales too long. Kendra has long hair that takes all the colors of the sun, a gentle voice, deep penetrating eyes, to say nothing of fine breasts and hips. I know that I will be thinking of her out of all relation to the actual role she will play in my life here. Eldridge, I think, might understand this; he showed an amused consciousness of my disturbance as I was introduced to her, and kept giving her sidelong glances as she played with her horse in the backyard, paused to help Mrs. Eldridge bring us drinks now and then, but he is a man of great reserve and said nothing. Why should he?

Eldridge, in answer to Hubbs's queries, pointed out that they had started pulling out of Paradise City about three or four weeks past, first just a few, then almost all of the residents together. The lemming effect. It was the ants that had discouraged them, of course, but the actual damage inflicted by them, Eldridge went on, most of it anyway, had occurred after the project had been abandoned, which meant that if they had resolved to stay and fight as Eldridge had, the ants would have posed little problem. He did not seem bitter, however. "People hate *ants,*" he said. "There's something about them that just disgusts most of us, but Clete and I we aren't too bothered. I don't think of them as animals, but as a kind of vegetation, and what the hell can you do with vegetation except to control it and clear it away? No," he said, "I don't think that we're going to have any trouble now," just a-setting and a-rocking. Kendra's horse whickered, Clete begged pardon and went back to do some more ditch-digging. "Maybe," Eldridge said, "it was just too much heat for them, these people I mean. Most of them aren't really desert types, you know; they're city dwellers with sinus problems who got conned into paying a few thousand for some property they'd never seen. They were looking for any excuse to go. I don't hold nothing against them," he said again. "But what I don't like is that when we get the ants cleared away I'm going to have to do the rebuilding practically single-handed. Most of them are never going to be back."

"We're from the National Science Foundation," Hubbs said. "We'll give you plenty of assistance, you can be sure of that. And afterward there should be a grant for rebuilding."

"Maybe," Eldridge said with the air of a man who had seen both too much and too little government in his time, his suspicion not personal—he liked Hubbs, after all—but radiating as a kind of absent contempt. "And then again maybe not. Only thing that brings people into the Arizona desert is they think they can get something out of it easy; project developers, scientists looking for giant ants, but who's going to stay? I'm going to stay."

"There are a lot of collapsed houses around here," I pointed out, perhaps irrelevantly, but trying to establish some part in the conversation. Somehow my potential connection to Kendra, I decided, could only be established through Eldridge; I would have to establish a relationship with him in order to reach her . . . juvenile thinking perhaps, but I had a strange feeling of hesitancy about the girl. "Maybe they had their reasons to run."

"I really wouldn't know about that," Eldridge said. "Like I said, I didn't pay much attention to any of them. They came from the city mainly and they're heading right back there. I've got to hold my ground. This is my place."

"Ah," Hubbs said. "But what about the towers?"

Eldridge squinted; the complexion of his face changed. "I don't know anything about the towers," he said.

"Well, you must have seen—"

"I just don't know anything about them," Eldridge said. "I *seen* them and I know what you're talking about, but mostly I don't think about them. What's the point of it?" A practical man.

"Do you think there's any connection between the towers and the ants?" Hubbs said.

This was the key question; one that had been weaving around in my subconscious for several hours now, and hearing it, dredged it to the surface like a drowned body; I felt, in fact, a kind of nausea. Of course, of course, there had to be some connection, it was obvious; the growth of the towers, the growth of the ants. Hubbs had been able to see it and make that connection easily, whereas I had been afraid

33

to . . . but Eldridge merely nodded, his face still bearing that strange, implacable expression, and said, "I don't know about that either." He paused. "Of course, it's been a dry year. You know, you can get ants in dry years. I once talked to an entomologist at the State Department of Agriculture and he said that these things were cyclical."

"He wasn't talking about ants," Mildred pointed out matter of factly. She had been inside the house, but now at Eldridge's invitation—"Come out and meet these people; lest they think I've got you chained up in that house"—she joined us, nodding again.

"These are university people," Eldridge said to her. "They're going to develop a new spray for those ants. Give us some help. Of course I think the ditches will do the trick, but you never know; we can always use some reinforcements."

"You know what I think?" Mrs. Eldridge said.

"Don't tell them," Eldridge said.

"I want to."

"Stop worrying," he said harshly. His whole expression had changed. So had Mildred's. They were not *American Gothic* anymore but something out of Breughel. "Leave these people alone with your ideas."

She shook her head and Hubbs made then what I think was a serious mistake, but there is no way of rectifying or even going back to it now. He took a sheet of paper out of his pocket, read some bureaucratese at them, and said that they were being evacuated. Eldridge reacted with shock. So did I. I hadn't even known that he was carrying such an order around with him. Full of surprises, my senior associate.

"Now look here," Eldridge said, and now we were no longer a-setting and a-rocking, but all of a sudden we were confronting. I looked for Kendra, but she had gone way off into the back, and in some illustration of the pathetic fallacy, the sun had clouded over. "Look here," this sixty-five-year-old man said. "What's this all about anyway? This isn't right; they can't push us off our own—"

"It's necessary," Hubbs said. His pedantry had returned; it seemed that all of the setting and rocking had only been a brief, pastoral interval after all. "For your own protection. Some very dangerous insecticides and other preparations are going to be used here, and they might pose a real threat to you; you can certainly return—"

"The ditches," Eldridge said. "We have ditches, we have oil, now listen to me doctor whoever you are, this is our land and—"

"Hubbs," he said. "Ernest D. Hubbs. Now look, Mr. Eldridge, I said that I'm truly sorry about this. It isn't my doing; it's a governmental order, and believe me you'll be much happier not being exposed or exposing your family to our righting of the balance here." Eldridge's face had turned orange in color now, his movements were somewhat feebler as he got out of the chair. "I'm sorry," Hubbs said, perhaps thinking that Eldridge was going to attack him, raising hands to face. "But—"

"Listen," Mildred said, taking Eldridge by the hand. "The man is right; don't you see that? He's right; we can't go on this way. The ants," she said and Eldridge's face was not the only one turning color now. There was a true festival of color on the porch, except that Mildred's was a bright green. "The *ants*—" she said and attempted to go on, but couldn't. She seemed to choke and as she did Eldridge's expression altered altogether, his fury became despair and he seemed to collapse; it was as if air was going out of him, he collapsed in small stages, sitting on the chair, and Mildred took his hand while Hubbs watched with astonishment, nonplused being the word I suppose, although I doubt if nonplusment is a part of Hubbs's range of behavior.

"It's for our own protection," Eldridge said softly, clutching her. "All right, then. We'll go."

I looked to Hubbs for some confirmation of my own astonishment—never have I seen such an alteration so quickly—but he was looking out toward the desert, his eyes shadowed.

"For our own protection," Eldridge repeated.

I looked for Kendra, but could not see her.

IV

"All right," Lesko said, driving the jeep. "That's good enough. But when do they get their farm back?"

"That depends," Hubbs said. Little marks of strain appeared on his forehead. "Among other things it depends on when we can clear out the ants, doesn't it?"

"That was rough," Lesko said. He felt obscurely angry, but was unable, somehow, to penetrate that anger; he knew that it had nothing to do with Hubbs. "The old man may be the last survivor. He's holding out."

"That doesn't concern me," Hubbs said. "We've got a job to do."

"You didn't have to spring the evacuation order on him. That was rough. You could have worked your way into it."

"I'm not in the social sciences," Hubbs said. His face was very tense now, and sweat was coming off it freely. "I'm not a psychiatrist or a social worker; I'm an ecologist with background in biophysics."

"All right," Lesko said.

"And what are you, Mr. Lesko? You're a researcher in game theory. By your own admission, not mine mind you, you're strictly a pencil and paper man; you don't deal with people."

"I said all right," Lesko said. His hands were very tight on the wheel. In the distance, off to the right, he could see the towers, and the uncomfortable feeling was rising in his chest again, soaking through his stomach and bowels. He did not know how much longer he could keep on driving, could keep on being matter of fact about the situation. It was bizarre, that was all, entirely bizarre, and the afternoon with Eldridge, which had started out so promisingly, had ended by making him ill. "Let's forget the whole thing."

"It's the girl," Hubbs said. His voice was flat and quite even. "You're thinking about that girl. Well, Lesko, you're a healthy, normal young man; you're certainly entitled to such interests, and she is a charming little thing. But if you think that that can interfere—"

"Hubbs," Lesko said very quietly, slowing the vehicle. "I want you to keep quiet now. I want you to shut up. If you don't, I can't tell you what I might do. You asked for me and I'm here at your request; we have to work together and I'm willing to do it . . . but I don't want to hear you mention the girl

37

again." Little blots of color were coming out on his cheeks; abruptly he looked much older than thirty-five. The vehicle was now completely at rest. "Do you hear me?" he said. "Do you hear me now?"

"All right," Hubbs said in a shaken voice. "I hear you."

"That's good," Lesko said. He put the jeep back in gear again, and they started to roll. Hubbs sat shrunken in one corner, staring out over Lesko's shoulder at the desert, his eyes clouded. A hand trembled as he raised it to wipe sweat from his forehead.

"I mean that," Lesko said.

This thing is already getting to me, he thought, and it's going to destroy me unless I'm careful.

The towers glinted at them.

V

The towers had been waiting for this, and now at last it had come. The signals were clear and strong; contact was being attempted. The creatures had at last acknowledged their existence, and in one way or the other were trying to bridge the gap of communication. All was as had been scheduled. Everything was moving along.

The queens in a stupor that was and was not conscious, revolved slowly, empty eyes staring into the darkness. Somewhere grids clicked; a series of impulses began, and those impulses coded toward a new level. Eggs began to drop limpidly from the bodies of the queens at a faster rate.

Everything was in order now. Everything was proceeding as it should.

Patiently, the towers waited.

VI

"I'm not going to go," Eldridge said a little later. "I can't. I've got my life here."

"You shouldn't," Kendra said. She had come back to the house after the scientists had left and had needed to hear little from Mildred or see much of her grandfather before she knew what had happened. "I'll stay with you."

"I know why you'll stay with him," Mildred said dryly. "You want to stay around where that younger one is. That Lesko, was that his name?"

Eldridge looked at his granddaughter and saw her faint blush. "No harm in that," he said. "I'll take her under any conditions. I need her. I need both of you. I want to stay."

"These aren't usual ants," Mildred said. "Don't you realize that?"

"I try not to realize anything," Eldridge said. He stood and walked to the door, looked out at the landscape, now deceptively quiet under the sunset. "Mostly I just go on."

"What are they planning to do?" Kendra said. "Hubbs and Lesko I mean."

"Apparently they're working with computers of some sort," Eldridge said. "Computers and insecticides. Maybe the computers are whipping up a batch of insecticide for all I know. I'm not a technical man; I don't know what the hell computers do these days. But they want to use some sophisticated devices to get at the problem."

"They don't even know what the problem is," Mildred said softly.

"I know what it is," Eldridge said grimly. "It's a lot of ants, that's what it is. Killer ants. There was an incident like this in South America not so many years ago, and they had to burn up a hundred square miles of countryside to get rid of them, but they did. They did it. I've got ditches and oil, and I'll do the same goddamned thing. They're not going to take over this place. I've backed out of everything else, but this is my life, and I've made my stand here." He was trembling. "Goddamned ants," he said.

"All right," Kendra said. She went to the old man and took his hand. "All right. Don't get emotional. We're all going to stay."

"This is my goddamned *life*," Eldridge said. "Doesn't anyone understand that?"

He looked out at the desert.

Surely it was a trick of light, but something seemed to be stirring out there.

VII

Lesko's Diary: Two days in here and I can see that this is not going to be a ten-day job. Or a two-week job or a three-week job or even necessarily a two-month job. We are in here for the duration. Already I have that same murky feeling about the station that long-term enlisted men have about their barracks, the feeling that long-married men have about their hated wives. This is my *life*. This is what *contains* me. Meanwhile, Hubbs continues with insane cheerfulness.

The thing is that the ants have not made an appearance. The terrain has been absolutely quiet since we settled in here, almost as if they were watching us and had decided to reconnoiter. (Is this paranoia? Am I ascribing an intelligence to the ants that they do not possess? I would not know this; for one thing, I have never *seen* them.) Hubbs plays with his computers; the stylographs whisk out geometric patterns that essentially indicate that nothing is being received; the corps of engineers, having dropped hardware, software, provisions, and reading materials on us, have taken off to the west, gratefully no doubt, leaving us to our own devices. Because there is absolutely no research or deductions I can make in the complete absence of data, I have spent these forty-eight hours verging toward an insanity compounded of boredom, an insanity in no way helped by the fact that I continue to feel that there is something peculiarly ominous going on here that we do not understand. The towers for one thing. But Hubbs is perfectly content. He has arrived at what no doubt is his ideal situation. He has a sterile, aseptic environment, a young male associate who he regards only as furniture, his comforting computers, printouts, readouts, binary codes, and speculations, and all the empty space any man could ever need. Not so much as a single feeling or emotion could threaten him in this situation . . . unless, of course, the ants march. So far they have not. For all I know, the whole series of reports and findings may be the deliberate imaginings of land developers who, faced with a dying property, decided to produce a little mass hysteria in order to evacuate the land and collect their insurance. If they have insurance. This is an idea.

Eldridge is holding out. I know this, for this morning I saw Kendra riding on her horse past the station; I also saw in the distance Clete on the tractor, kicking up more sand clouds as he continued to work on his ditches. Kendra seemed to linger for a moment toward the rear, and for a moment I thought of going out and speaking to her, reaching a hand, inviting her in, holding her, telling her what I thought . . . any number, in short, of foolish, insane gestures that would have converted a difficult situation into an impossible one. I cannot allow my emotional state to interfere with the business of this project, whatever it is, and although I am touched deeply by this girl in ways that I cannot even know, the fact is that I have barely spoken to her, she exists only in my mind . . . and furthermore I have no desire to incur Hubbs's wrath. I am working under him; we must get along. I know instinctively that he would be infuriated were I to attempt a relationship with this girl, and he would be right. For one thing, Eldridge is under government order to vacate this area along with his family, which means that I would be consorting—would I not? —with a felon.

Hubbs knows that Eldridge is holding out, of course, but he has obviously decided, at least for the moment, to make nothing of it. He has his computers to keep him busy; also I think that he is obsessed with the idea that the ants may appear outside or within the station at any moment to launch a vicious attack. He wants to be ready for them, hardly sidetracked in the subissue that Eldridge's eviction would surely be. Besides that, and to look at this perfectly objectively, what could Hubbs do if Eldridge defied him? (Which Eldridge already has, although circuitously, of course.) Eldridge is sixty-five, but a tough old bastard for all of that, and although Clete might even be a little older, he has the aspect of a man who knows how to handle a rifle and probably has a few stashed away in that tractor of his. Would a fifty-year-old laureate from the Coronado Institute be willing to take on two tough old southwestern geezers, particularly in the presence of women who might not be entirely sympathetic to this? I can follow this line of argument myself, so surely Hubbs can. I have a certain sympathy for his position, although, of course, it is quite limited.

One side of the station is close to the towers, no more than fifty yards I would suspect and has an excellent if rather dismal view of them. Through the plastic and shading of the windows, they do not appear nearly so ominous; the peculiar quality of light and graining that so disturbs me is filtered out . . . but they are large, they are very large, and I cannot escape the feeling, somehow, that they are still growing. The computer installation, of course, is now looking out on the towers, and this evening, for lack of anything better to do (I may be a game theorist, but I cannot abide solitaire, cryptograms, crossword puzzles, chess problems, or any of the million devices men use to avoid time; I would rather commit myself fully to suffering), I went into the installation and I found Hubbs, looking acutely frustrated, working over the computer. As he turned toward me, I saw his face showed far more expression and anger than I might have judged, and his eyes were absolutely bleak. It occurred to me that he was infuriated, and this time with no abstraction; it was the ant colony itself that was enraging Hubbs. Certainly no human could bring him to the level of loathing that these ants had. He did not even greet me; he simply took my entrance as inevitable at that time. "Can you believe this?" he said, pointing above him to a transmitter hooked in to the corps of engineers. "They want an itinerary, of all the damned things."

"There has already been an overrun," a voice said over the transmitter, as filtered out and dead through the machinery as the color of the towers through glaze. "And that overrun averages out at thirty-six percent when projected over the course of the total program. The comptroller would like to get the final figure before the fiscal period ends on the fourteenth."

Hubbs picked up a microphone and pressed a button. "I'm sorry, this is not a precise business," he said. He took his finger off the button and said to me, "Maybe you'd like to talk to them. You might have powers of reasoning that are beyond me."

"You've got to give us an estimate," the implacable voice said. "Surely you can do that, no?"

"We cannot," Hubbs said with great weariness, holding the microphone as if it weighed several pounds, "study these ants until they make an appearance."

"Ah," the voice said. "Then can we put you down for ten days more? A week? This is a matter of getting a proper cost-estimate. You must realize that overrides are budgetary calculations that simply must be integrated at every step of the line. We cannot arrange for an override unless—"

"Listen," Hubbs said, emotion flooding his voice. I felt sympathy for him, but not a great deal as I looked past him out at the towers, soft now in the sunset. If only they would go away, if only the accursed ants would come out, if only the desert would explode. Kendra kiss me . . . this was not a profitable course of speculation. "This is not a controlled experiment," Hubbs was saying. "Our best judgment indicates another occurrence in this area is highly probable. But we cannot command the ants to appear. We have not established communication with them."

"Well," the voice said, "is there something that you might be able to do to hurry them up?"

Hubbs held the microphone and looked up at the transmitter for a while with a curiously calculating expression. "We've been thinking about that," he said.

"You know there's some concern over possible outbreaks in other areas," the transmitter said.

"Yes," Hubbs said. His features coalesced; abruptly he looked rather determined. "I think that my associate, Mr. Lesko, might have something to say to you," he said and passed the microphone over to me. Then he reached above the computer, took some-

45

thing off a shelf . . . and, opening the near door, walked out into the desert.

"What is this?" the voice said. "What is going on there? Mr. Lesko?" But all I could do was stand there, microphone in hand, rather dumfounded I must admit and also possessed with a sudden, exact understanding of what Hubbs was going to do. "Wait a minute," I said into the microphone and then realized that I had forgotten to press the button. "Just wait a minute," I said, this time speaking into it, and then I flung the microphone from myself with some force, feeling a dread that went beyond even the possibility of verbalization, and sprinted out into the night, the transmitter yammering, the stylus of the computer twitching out its odd little signals and there—

—I saw Hubbs holding a hand-grenade launcher, and even as I ran toward him he fired off the first egg-shaped missile toward the near tower. The grenade hit high, one or two feet from the top, and instantly there was fire and fragmentation; in that fire a halo of splinters and then the tower was open, the top of it toppling behind to the sand, and *from the tower a blackness of ooze was coming*—

"There," Hubbs said, his voice curiously dead and controlled. "That should hasten things right along. You see," he said turning to me calmly, the grenade launcher held easily at his side, he might have been a man in a bar holding a drink and calmly, dispassionately discussing the events of the day, "they're quite right back at the base, despite the fact that their attitudes are patronizing. We can't go on this way, Lesko, we've got to get some action out of this, because I have no intention of spending the rest of my life in the desert waiting for those filthy little cunning buggers to pick their time and place. We're *men*, we make our own conditions," and he raised the launcher again and got off another quick shot toward the open space of the tower. More shards in the air, more toppling, and then the ooze, heaving like a river, was pouring down the sides.

My first instinct was that Hubbs had gone entirely mad, but in an acceleration of time and insight, looking at the horror pouring out of there, I became aware that he was not mad, not at all. He had only done a logical, reasonable thing to bring events to confrontation . . . and if, in some way, the ants were observing us, charting our patterns, then he had been particularly cunning in seizing the launcher and making a frontal attack without any preparation whatsoever. It was the kind of random activity that in game theory is absolutely compelling; in just such a way can an amateur occasionally beat a chess master or at least seriously menace him . . . by making the wrong moves, by not being predictable. Staring at what was coming out of the towers as Hubbs fired one more shot, I found myself admiring the man; he was not such a dead, decayed abstraction after all, but rather one of a certain force and courage that had led him to perform precisely that act that I would have if I had had the authority . . . and the imagination. Hubbs threw the launcher from him out into the desert and went back inside; I followed him. He closed the door and bolted it. Then he turned to me, his face happier than I had ever seen it, and he went back to the computer board.

"Now we'll see some action," he said.

VIII

Kendra must have been sleeping when it began, although later she could not think of it as sleep; rather it had been some dull, cylindrical passage of time, unconsciousness perhaps, no dreams, nothing but a traversal of fear (it had been like this for her since the ants came), and then she came fully awake to the screaming of her horse. The filly, tethered outside, was screaming as she had never heard it before; a human scream, a child's scream, with a note of blood and terror in it that she could not, could never have associated with an animal. She was out of bed instantly, fighting with the window, tearing open the shade, and looking out there. Her only thought was for the filly; she must somehow save it from its agony. Rearing to seven or eight feet, the horse was frantic, eyeballs rolling, hooves clattering against the posts, and then Kendra saw what had happened to the horse. Ants hung from the body in little distended clumps that at first she took for welts or growths, ants nesting together, biting at the animal; and as the horse reared, a shower of ants fell like a waterfall, translucent, filtering toward the ground, the horse screaming. Kendra screamed too, breath fighting for release in her throat, screamed and lunged at the window; her only impulse was to get to the horse, but now lights were going on all through the house, and she was

48

battering herself against the wall, helpless, her need to get to the filly overwhelmed by shock. Breath moved unevenly in her lungs, and then as she felt a tingling at the calves, she screamed, slapped down there, watching a small, spreading smear of red.

Ants. They were on her.

"Clete!" Her grandfather was shouting from the next room. "Clete, they're here!" His bellow showed less surprise than the confirmation of something long expected, and there was, she thought with horror, something joyous in it. *He's glad; he's glad they're coming.* She turned, her only thought now to get out of the room, and something caught her by the wrists, pulled her through the door, and shoved her against the outer wall. "Kendra!" her grandfather said. "Are you all right?" He was holding a rifle.

"The horse!" she said. "They've got my horse!"

"I know," Mildred said, coming from her own bedroom. "They're here!"

"Please," Eldridge said, holding Kendra still in that one-hand grasp, the other shoving the rifle barrel at the floor. "Please, you've got to be calm. There isn't anything we can do—"

But she broke free of him then, screaming *Ginger!* her strength demoniac out of terror, and she burst through the living room, flung open the door, and ran into the yard. Somewhere Clete ran past her carrying his own rifle, his eyes glaring and terrified. A cluster of insects seemed to be on his shirt, or perhaps Kendra was only seeing this in her panic and terror. The horse: that was all that mattered, she had to get to the horse. It was not that Ginger meant so much to her, although she meant enough; it was that she could not take the suffering, the idea that the animal was in such pain. *I didn't know you cared so much,*

a cool mad internal voice advised her. Behind her
she heard her grandfather and Clete calling to one
another, shouting orders; they seemed to want to
light the oil in the ditches. In the darkness she did not
know what was underneath her feet; all she knew was
that she was able to keep her balance. Mildred was
screaming in a high wail of terror and doom; fire sput-
tered, missed, and then with a *whoomp!* one of the
ditches went up, spilling fragments of flaming oil, arc-
ing them into the sky. Kendra fumbled with the
gate and got into the corral. The filly had reared up
against a post and stood there now in frieze, its eyeballs blackened with the forms of ants. It was quivering through the skeleton and involuntary muscles, but
was otherwise poised and quiet. Kendra did not know
what to do. The filly looked at her without recognition.
Shoot it. That was what you were supposed to do, of
course: get a rifle and shoot it. She had never touched
a firearm. How could you shoot another living thing,
no matter how it was suffering? It was still murder.
More fires went up, the glaze of fire lighting the corral to the pitch of day. Her grandfather and grandmother appeared at the fence, their faces illumined
and streaked by the fire.

"Wait," her grandmother said. "We'll do something."

"No," Kendra said. "No!"

"Get me the gun," Eldridge said, and Mildred
went away, came back in a moment holding a rifle
uncertainly. She passed it over to Eldridge. He took it
and checked the barrel.

"No!" Kendra said. "You can't do it!"

"It's got to be done," Eldridge said. "I was wrong.
We should have left when they told us to."

"You can't shoot my horse," Kendra said.

"There's no other way," said Eldridge. He pointed the rifle. Clete appeared in the middle of this, looked at the horse, then at Kendra, his eyes wide and confused. *"Where are the little bastards?"* he said. *"Everything's on fire."*

"Get her in the house," Eldridge said.

Clete came toward her hesitantly. "Don't kill her!" Kendra screamed. "Don't kill my horse!" And the screams whipped Clete into action as pleas, probably, would not; he seized her by the arms and began to tug her through the gate. The filly was screaming again now, struggling against the post. Kendra fought free of Clete desperately, but only for an instant; then he had her wrapped up in his arms again, and she felt a curious, absent passion almost as if she and the hired man were lovers and in the next moment he was going to penetrate her. *Insanity.* She pushed him away with a last effort of will, and then allowed him to drag her by the hand toward the house. "What are they going to do to her?" she said.

"You know what they're going to do."

"They can't!" she said, but she did not try to resist him this time. She left her hand in his. "They can't do it!"

"They're going to take care of her," Clete said. "It's got to be this way." And then they were inside the house, and as the light from the ditches flared up, Kendra saw it fully and screamed again.

Ants were all through the house. The fire must have driven them from the safety of the earth; now they had enveloped the beams, the ceiling, the walls . . . even as she watched, stiff with shock, pieces of ceiling plaster collapsed under the weight of ants, shattering on the floor, the struggling forms scattering with the impact. Clete, stunned, reached out a foot and stamped on one clump of ants, then another, a slow shuffle step. Kendra thought that she might be laughing. She did not want to put a hand to her mouth to verify. Better not to know certain things; all that she did know was that she had to get out of this house. More plaster dropped, rattled, squirming little things scuttled from it, some of them moving across her shoetips. Suddenly she felt herself weightless, being lifted from the floor and through the thick air of the house, and she screamed again, feeling as if it were a blanket of ants that had somehow appropriated her, but no, it was Clete, his face close to hers. "I'm getting you out," he said. "Please, don't scream; we're getting out." His face was stricken and youthful in the light. She tried to show him that she understood, that she knew he was trying to help her, but no words would come. And then she was being tossed, roughly but precisely, over the tailgate of the truck, Clete vaulting behind her. They were in the back of the pickup. Eldridge, at the wheel, leaned over, looked through the open panel. "Is she all right?" he said.

"I'm all right," Kendra said and stretched out on the wood. "I'll be all right."

"Let's get out of here," Mildred said, and Eldridge turned back to the wheel. Kendra felt a terrific force shoving her against the panels, and then the truck was in flight, Clete supporting her, bumping and rolling down the road. Fires illuminated their path; in the fires, she could see the black forms struggling. Some of them seemed airborne. Groups of them slapped against the slats of the truck like birds. "It's all right," Clete said again. "We're getting out. We're going to be all right."

"Is Ginger dead?"

"Yes," he said. "She didn't suffer. She's dead."

52

"We should have gotten out of here when they told us."

"Too late now."

"Why didn't we listen?"

"Nobody listens ever," Clete said. "Listening isn't human. Be calm. We'll leave now."

"The ants would listen," she said crazily. "They talk to one another. They don't have to argue. They just *know.*"

"I forgot to turn off the lights," Mildred said through the front. Hearing this made Kendra laugh; she began to laugh almost hysterically until Clete soothed her by rubbing her back. They were out of range of the fires now; the road illuminated only by their headlights ... and then Mildred screamed.

Kendra reared to attention, Clete's arm dropping from her, and Mildred screamed again, a shorter, more piercing note, a high bark. Looking through the open panel, Kendra saw what had made her grandmother scream, and if she had had the voice left, she would have screamed too ... but she could only gasp. Ants were all over her grandfather's head. They had formed a net over his white hair, they had worked their way in jagged little clumps into his ears, they were down his neck, spinning onto his shirt ... she fell straight back in the pickup, striking her head on the planks.

Clete, bellowing, was trying to get through the opening, to take the wheel himself, but he could not. The opening was too small; he battered himself against it, wailing. The truck, now completely out of control, lurched off the roadway and onto the naked desert, the wheels breaking into a long, jagged slide, the truck weaving in patterns that no vehicle could make and yet remain on four wheels. Kendra, half-conscious, gripped the planks feeling all sensation depart. Mildred's screaming continued, but in this altered perspective Kendra found it almost pleasant; if the world was ending, as it surely was, better with screams than submission . . . Clete was bellowing and kicking at the slats, trying to free himself. For a moment it seemed that he might make it, drop to the sands of the desert, and at least get free—and Kendra was glad; Clete owed her nothing, and he was entitled to a fight for survival if he could maintain it—but the truck was moving crazily at angles to itself and the sky that it could not sustain . . . and Kendra lay back, pinned by the gravity, watching Clete's struggles like those of an insect on a pin. The truck rolled sickeningly, yawed to one side . . . and then with the kind of magnificent certainty that can only come, she thought, from complete disaster, it broke entirely free of the ground, rolled through the air in an abbreviated flight that seemed to last for an interminable length of time . . . and then as her consciousness vaulted to embrace the fact of her death, of her grandparents' deaths, of the death of everything that she had had so briefly and now lost . . . the truck hit something, was embraced in a sheet of flame. She waited for the explosion. Surely it was coming. Then it came.

IX

"You see," Hubbs said to Lesko when they were once more in the station, "what I've done is very interesting."

"You shouldn't have shot the towers," Lesko said weakly. "You just shouldn't have—"

"But I had to," Hubbs said in a positive professorial tone. "You see, what I've done is to get at the parameters of the problem by breaking down the movements of a vector of a single ant unit."

He motioned to the figures that the stylus of the computer was implacably tracking out, singing all the time to itself. "They've changed, you see," he said. "I've broken down their simple, obvious movements, and the whole pattern of the colony has changed. You can see that the overall refraction of the agglomeration of movements is now represented by a bell curve rather than a wave line. That is extraordinarily interesting."

Lesko backed against one of the walls. "You shouldn't have done it," he said again. "You don't know. We don't know the quality of the things in those towers; we can't understand—"

"We couldn't have waited," Hubbs said with that same curious precision. "You're not the only one who wants to get out of the desert; I have feelings too, you know. This is a mission to be completed in a minimum amount of time, and now we're making strides. Look at the ant signals," he said, tearing the paper off the roller with a flourish. "The whole pattern has changed. Assumption, Lesko: what we are seeing and hearing on the printout are commands directing the movements of the mass. Okay?"

"Probably," Lesko said dully. He looked out through the windows and saw the broken clumps falling from the towers. Hubbs had hurt them, yes . . . *but what were they going to do now?* "We're not denying that there is a level of communication among the creatures."

"Good," Hubbs said. He made marks on the paper; he might have been instructing a class. "Now what we are seeing and hearing then are commands, and I can make various adjustments to take care of the time lag and some other things. Don't worry about that." He was moving the pencil swiftly now, caught in a computational ecstasy. "I find something," he said.

"What?"

"Do you know what? I find a positive correlation on the order of eighty percent between this squiggle—" he took the paper and put it abruptly in Lesko's hands, who looked at it as Hubbs's pen point traced out the finding— "a correlation between that squiggle, and a command that we might generally verbalize as *stop.*" He pointed at another arc on the paper. "And there is also a positive correlation between this little squiggle and *movement.* Do you know what that means, Lesko," he said. He whipped off his glasses and stared, his eyes little points of light through which things flickered. "Do you see what we're getting at now?"

"I think so."

"It means that the sons of bitches are talking to one another," Hubbs said, and the lights in the station went out.

X

Lesko's Diary: I will give Hubbs credit; he did not panic. When we lost power in the station, this incident directly connected in my mind with the assault upon the towers, I felt that the fundamental imbalance that I had felt about the situation since it began was now asserting itself. To put it another way (I must learn to phrase these matters as simply as possible; scientific jargon or convoluted rhetoric will get me nowhere, and I must relate the facts as straightforwardly as possible), I was sure that the ants, crippled by the damage to the tower, had now regrouped and were striking back with vicious force; the first part of the attack, of course, being the cutting of our power. Helplessness overwhelmed me; instantly it seemed ten degrees hotter as the hum of the air conditioners, the whine of the computer bank, the yammering of the speaker all stopped at once, and atavistic panic came over me in great waves. *Night,* I must have screamed, *we are stranded in eternal night,* or some such nonsense, and it was Hubbs, putting a steady hand on my wrist, who brought me back to myself. "It's all right," he said. Close against me, he was visible in the dim light streaking through the windows, and as my eyes began to re-adjust, I now glimpsed the station whole again. "It's all right. Now we know that they're hurt. They're coming out," he said. "Let's get them."

"Get them?"

"Get them," he said. "We're going to paint them yellow, the filthy little sons of bitches," his tones quite cheerful and confident. He guided me toward a rack on which our full-protection gear hung: helmets, outer suits, masks, breathing apparatus, all making us look as if we were preparing for a walk on the moon, not the benign Arizona desert. As Hubbs began very calmly and methodically to work himself into one, I felt myself stricken with admiration for the man: truly he had anticipated this necessity. The suits were required gear of course, but it had been he who had thought of hanging them toward the side of the station within reach. I joined him there, clambering into the gear, and as I zipped up the blank, thick surfaces of the suit and clamped the helmet and inhalator into place, I had a feeling that only a naked man stranded streetside and then thrown a merciful blanket must feel . . . I was coming back to myself, piece by shaken piece as I put on the gear. As we were making our final adjustments, the power came back with a roar, lights to bright, the computer making up for its brief sleep with a grateful *whoomp!* of greeting, making up for lost time as well with a frantic series of printouts pouring out of the rollers as if the computer, no less human than we, had been embarrassed by its failure. Behind his mask, Hubbs looked as foreign as any of the towers, but his voice through the facespeaker was quite flat and calm, and as I listened, it was as if I could still see that smile of his. "Let's put on the yellow," he said again, and charged toward the safety switches.

"Shouldn't we wait?" I said. "Maybe—" and with a solemn relevance, the power went off again. The lights faded, the computer gave a disgusted *whap!* and was silent, left in the middle of a printout that looked vaguely like an obscene doodle. Hubbs was already working on switches fired by the emergency generator implanted deep underground, and around the station I could see a fine, yellow mist rising, already coating everything in the colors of the sun. The towers yellow, the sands yellow, the windows yellow, my own gloved hand yellow. Hubbs's hands were slap, slapping at the switches. Nozzles extended from the station to throw long-range bombs of insecticide into the desert.

P-2 or PX-2, some chemical insecticide, I was not clear on the name, leaving that business to Hubbs, who is, of course, the biologist and killer-expert. My own area has given me a happy immunity to technology; I could not give the chemical formula for water, nor have I ever felt a personal or educational emptiness because I could not schematize the formulae for those interesting poison gases that could destroy half the population in a trice. No, it was sufficient for me to know that P-2 or PX-2 was doing the job; its effectiveness could not be questioned. Not only were we plunged into a world of yellow that in other, less grim circumstances might have had a kind of gaiety (a million daffodils rising through harsh grasses, the sun beaming lushly through a meadow), but the ants were obviously in dire straits. I could see huge clumps of them, soldered together into necklaces, falling like rain past the windows; tumbling from all parts of the station where they had previously taken up a precarious position; black forms

were rapidly being coated with yellow and were writhing and twisting like dancers on the sands, and Hubbs
himself was in an ecstasy of happiness. "That does
it!" he was shouting, his voice no longer flat. Mechan-
ical reduction or not, the pleasure this gave him rang
through. "Let's go out and do the finishing touches
ourselves!" and he seized off the wall a small, flat
spray can, a kind of Portable Yellow, handed it to
me, took another for himself, and led me out into the
desert. Instantly the doors had been closed, the locks
cleared; he pointed his spray before him, and the
aerosol can sent huge, lazy spurting jets of yellow into ground before him.

Seen this way, the desert was curiously beautiful.
The nozzles had projected the insecticide through
an area of several hundred square yards, perhaps
more than that; throughout the whole range of vi-
sion, in any event, the world was coated with a mer-
ry yellow, broad, happy streaks of yellow being
painted across the landscape, and like flies in gelatin,
crumbs on a coffee cake, little black heaps were em-
bedded in the yellow, flakes falling like snow upon
it, turning black into yellow, ants into artifacts even as
we watched. "This is the end," Hubbs said. "Now
we can go home." And holding his spray gun as a
drunken conductor might handle a baton, he danced
out on the desert, bellowing in what must have been
song. I followed him; he sprinted down the roadway,
firing random little bursts, more ants wherever we
looked, and then as we rounded a little corner, turned
a little rise, we saw something—

—We saw an overturned truck, human forms crawling from it, two of them waving feebly like drowned
insects, another lying quietly, and my first thought
was *where did a truck come from?* But in the next in-

stant, after that small interval of total stupidity, everything came clear, all of it bursting or yellowing in upon me, and I was sprinting ahead of Hubbs, running desperately, lungs burning in the insufficient air I could draw through the inhalator. The first body was that of Mrs. Eldridge. She was coated with yellow, only her eyes, pure black, stared through, her knees drawn up in a fetal position, one hand extended childlike, balled into a fist. I reached over to touch her and then instantly straightened, horrified. I started to walk toward the next body, terrified of who I might find fifty yards away, but was brought up by Hubbs's voice. He was not behind me. He had stopped at the truck and was squatting, looking at one of the wheels, which was still spinning, then squinting up into the exposed chassis. I went over to him, not because I wanted to see anything but because I dreaded what lay ahead. I knew. I knew that they were all dead.

"This is really fascinating," Hubbs said.

"Those are dead people over there."

"I know," Hubbs said, his gaze not shifting. "It's really a tragedy and I don't understand it. They heard the order. They accepted it. Why would they stay?"

"I don't know," I said. "Maybe they had nowhere else to go." I cannot remember what my exact emotional state was. I suppose I wanted to hit them, although this would have been irrelevant.

Yellow, he looked up at me. "Irrational behavior," he said. "It's really very sad, these so-called desert people. But James, look at this."

I leaned over. Perhaps he was going to show me his heart and with it some sense of what his purposes were, how he could be this way. But he was pointing at mounds of ants impacted well up into the chassis.

"Consider that," he said. "The execution of the maneuver . . . for this was clearly a maneuver. In order to create the spark—"

"Goddamn it all Hubbs," I said in a strange detachment that children must feel when they are being dragged away by their parents but must protest if only for dignity's sake. "Those people are dead, don't you understand? They're *dead*. The insecticide killed them."

"Well," Hubbs said, looking up into the chassis, extending a gloved finger to delicately brush some ants away from an exposed rod. "People do get killed sometimes, you know. Death is being killed itself; that happens to all of us."

"I don't understand you," I said to him, although of course I understood perfectly well; understanding was assaulting me in spokes of yellow no less brilliant than the landscape, and along with my revulsion, there was respect as well. I will admit this; it was impossible not to respect Hubbs, because it was *people like him who made the world work;* people who were able to shoot off the grenades, spread the insecticide, inspect the chassis, look at death dispassionately—they were the hope of the world, these people; Hubbs was the hope of the project because some agonized, sensitive types like myself, trapped in our delicate sensitivities and revulsions, would have been incapable of taking the strong, decisive action that Hubbs had taken. And if Hubbs seemingly was unable to feel, then this kind of insulation was probably necessary if you were going to get anything done. Most of the real accomplishments in the world were managed by people who had a lessened or negligible capacity to feel; they could not or would not be concerned with the pain of progress or battle, and therefore they could move ahead. This internal soliloquy, however, did not exactly exalt the spirits; it added a slow, mean edge to my despair, and, finding it necessary to get away from Hubbs at once, I scrambled to my feet and walked away from him down the road. He had given me courage, however: I was so mad at him that I believed that I could confront anything now without feeling.

Hubbs followed me, murmuring to himself. Seventy or eighty paces down the road, I saw the form of the hired man, Clete, lying half-concealed by tarpaulin that he had probably pulled from the truck in his death agonies, already shrouded as he had hit the ground, crawled a few feeble yards, and then died. I pulled away from the corpse as soon as I had identified it, but Hubbs, scooting up behind me, seized the tarpaulin and took it all the way down to the dead man's feet. He was covered with yellow right down to his shoes. Hubbs took a thin metal probe from a leg pouch and extended it toward the corpse's hand.

Fascinated, I will admit, I came back. All gesture fails with people like Hubbs; they are simply immune to any such display, and knowing that I had no power to affect him enabled curiosity to return. He nodded and poked away at the hand with the probe.

There was a small, neat hole about the size of a bullet hole in Clete's palm. Hubbs worked on it with the probe, one side to the other, and as we watched, three ants came marching out in close-order formation, *marche funèbre* the solemnity and precision of their movements grotesquely comical. They looked entirely purposeful as they turned to the left of the probe and continued their march, going into the sands. Hubbs took out a small container and put it over the ants. "Now," he said, "I guess that we can begin our researches." He picked up the filled container, sealed it over with a slide, and dropped it into his leg pouch again. "I know this may upset you, James," he said. "But you've got to realize that there was nothing to be done, nothing at all; if we had not used the insecticide, they might have taken over the station."

I guess that this was as close to an apology as Hubbs might get, in or out of this world, and I was just turning to tell him what I (and of course the entire company of decent, right-thinking people of this world) thought of him when, behind me, some yards down, I heard a horrid clash and creaking, and a truck door that I had not even noticed before, the yellow dust having amalgamated the whole landscape into a single color, came open, horrifyingly, inch by inch, and as I stared at it, paralyzed, unable to imagine what was coming out of it (I suppose that I thought it might be a giant ant), a figure covered with yellow staggered from the opening, weaved a step or two, and then, hand extended, collapsed on the sands in front of me.

Kendra.

I ran toward her and was about to seize her, embrace her against me, anything to get her out of here and relieve the agony, but it was Hubbs, coming up swiftly, who once again showed more sense. "Don't touch her," he said. "She's got to be covered." He pulled from another pouch some kind of canvas or burlap, yanking it out like a rope and then, furling it out against the yellow, dropped it over her body. He took her by the shoulders and motioned to me that I was to take her by the feet, and that was the way we got her out of there, a long, stumbling walk back toward the shelter, clouds of yellow coming off her in little puffs, but she was alive, alive: I could feel respiration, I could feel warmth; she had some-how survived, was going to live through the insecti-cide. I found myself thinking of course she would, *of course she would* in rhythm to our effort; she was younger than the other three, she had more resistance, and there was at least a chance that she would get through this. We would save her. We would get her back to the shelter, clean her, make her warm, aspi-rate the stuff out of her lungs in time, and bring her back to herself. . . .

But for what? dear God . . . and to what?

XI

After they had put the girl through the decontam-ination chambers, gotten her warm, gotten her into clothing, and placed her in a spare room of the sta-tion where she lay peacefully, not in coma but in a deep sleep, Hubbs and Lesko took off their own gear. Only then did Lesko take some measure of what these hours had done to him; he was trembling top to bot-tom, all of his body below the waist shaking so un-controllably that he could barely walk. "You've prob-ably taken in some of the fumes through the inhala-tor," Hubbs said matter of factly as he led them in-to the laboratory. "But I doubt if there'll be any lasting effects. The girl was out there, breathing P-2 for at least fifteen minutes, and she's going to be all right. Vital signs are normal."

"That's fine," Lesko said. "That changes every-thing, doesn't it?" But he was too tired, too shaken to argue with Hubbs. Hubbs was in command, and Les-ko had an almost childlike desire to keep that relation-ship now, for Hubbs was their only means of getting out of this. The man knew what he was doing or at least seemed to . . . whereas Lesko had literally lost the ability to deal with the situation. Through the windows of the laboratory they could see ants still floating through the air, dropping to the sands: most of them black, a few green ones intermixed, all with white bellies, falling like little paratroopers. "The little sons of bitches," Lesko said. "The dirty bas-tards."

"Don't personalize," Hubbs said, picking up a vial. "That won't do any good at all. They're not individ-uals. They're just individual cells, tiny functioning parts of a whole. Would you get mad at your cor-puscles if you had leukemia?"

"I hate them," Lesko said, and he thought, so do you; I heard you cursing them before, that was why you fired off the grenades, you son of a bitch, be-cause you couldn't take the situation anymore. So don't get scientific on me now . . . but he said noth-ing.

"Think of a society, James," Hubbs said. "A so-ciety with complete harmony, altruism, and self-sacrifice, perfect division of labor according to pre-ordained roles; think of the building of elaborate and complex structures according to plans they know noth-ing of . . . and yet execute perfectly. Think of their powers of aggression and their ability to evolve and adapt in ways that are so beautiful and still so un-known." His voice was almost reverent. "I've got to respect them," Hubbs said quietly. "It's all based on a simple form . . . so helpless in the individual. So powerful in the mass."

"In other words," Lesko said slowly, "it's a completely alternative approach to evolution."

"Go on, James."

"Well, it's obvious, isn't it? We've developed. The dominant species of the planet has developed through greater and greater individualization, isolation, but it could have gone the other way, couldn't it? You're talking about the ant gestalt in which only the pattern, the group, holds, the individual being a small cell of the mass. In that sense, the ants are immortal, aren't they? Individualization, the path we've taken, leads to greater and greater fragmentation and a terror of death as the loss of the individual consciousness. Whereas the ants would have no fear of death whatsoever; it would merely be the peeling off of one cell the way our own cells are supposed to die a million a day."

"That's almost profound, James," Hubbs said softly. "My faith in you was not misplaced after all. Yes, if you consider evolution as a series of choices, then it could have gone the other way. The ants could have been the dominant species—"

"And might yet be," Lesko said. "Is that the next step in the speculation? Maybe they're taking over now, fifty million years later."

Hubbs's face was very solemn. "Yes," he said. "I've thought of that." He shrugged, made a dismissive gesture. "Nevertheless," he said, "if that's true, it simply means that we must go on redoubled, eh? Surely they have no devices in comparison to the sophistication of ours; I'm afraid that they gave us too much time." He opened the vial, sniffed at it delicately, then put it on a rack. "Let's start with the

67

first behavorial series," he said and took the container that had been filled in the desert. "Heat, cold, starvation, isolation, slow squeezing—"

"Yes," Lesko said.

"Let's put some mantises on these ants," Hubbs said quietly, but with a tremor of anticipation under all of this. "Let's see what kind of signals we get."

Lesko said, "When are we going to get her out of here?"

"We're running some experiments."

Lesko shook his head. "Well and good," he said. "but we can't talk about comparable theories of evolution so easily. How are we going to get that girl out of here?"

Hubbs said, "That's going to be a bit difficult, isn't it? Turn on the microphones and the recorder, please."

"Why don't you call and have them send out a helicopter," Lesko said. "We're back in contact again."

Hubbs turned toward him and leaned on an elbow. "I would," he said. "I share your feelings of sympathy. But I don't think our bureaucrats would be too happy to know that we've had some fatalities. We'd be tied up in reports and explanations for days, and there are more important things to do." He turned back toward the sealed glass enclosure. "The mantises are at one end of our maze now," he said. "The ants at the other. . . ."

Lesko said, "What are we going to do with the girl, then? We've got to do something. She won't go away simply because you refuse to think of her, you know."

"What is your concern with her?" Hubbs said. "You're being wholly unprofessional about this, James."

68

"My concern is that she's in shock!" Lesko said loudly. "And we just cannot keep her here—"

"Don't shout at me," Hubbs said with deadly containment. "That is totally unnecessary." He paused, went back to the board, and then, as if still being prodded, said, "The girl, obviously, is a problem to be dealt with in a few days. After we've finished. We're making progress now, and we simply cannot be sidetracked."

"If you won't call the base," Lesko said quietly, "then I will."

"I'm very much afraid that that would end our mission. We would find ourselves swarming with personnel of the most odious type, and it would be impossible for us to complete our job here. We're not in human relations or social work, Lesko; we're involved in very difficult and, need I say, dangerous research here. This has become a very serious situation, and I don't think that we're out of the woods yet. The ants are entirely capable of gathering their remaining forces and striking yet again, and unless we are able to code out—"

"Forget our mission," Lesko said. He looked at Hubbs in a level, deadly way, and before this, Hubbs's eyes fell. Lesko stood, feeling the power coming into him. It all came down to physical intimidation, eventually. Everything was based upon that. Call it an outcome of the evolution of individualization: the stronger life-forms could intimidate the weaker. Implicit was the statement: *I can supplant you.*

"I'm going to call in," he said. "Do you want to argue with me about this?"

Hubbs said nothing.

Lesko turned, reached for the microphone, and

heard the door open behind him. Both men jumped, Hubbs actually reaching for the gun in his waistband. Kendra stood in the doorway, looking uneasy but back to herself. She was streaked here and there with lines that bore the shadows of yellow, her skin curiously opaque, but otherwise she looked merely tired. "I slept," she said. "Then after a while I didn't feel like sleeping anymore, so I got up. I remember everything. They're all dead, aren't they?"

"I guess so," Lesko said.

"They're all dead," Hubbs said at the console. "It's quite unfortunate, but they were warned."

"It occurred to me," she said to Lesko, ignoring Hubbs, "that I don't even know your name."

"My name is Jim Lesko. Jim. Come in," he said, motioning. "We're just starting to run some experiments, but it doesn't matter. We have a moment or two."

"We have nothing," Hubbs said, his mouth tight. "We have no time at all. Time is beyond us; we must hurry."

"I'll go," Kendra said.

"No," said Lesko. He hit the arm of his chair, indicating that she was not to move. "You had a very close call," he said gently.

"I remember," she said. "I told you—I remember everything."

"How are you feeling?"

"I'm ready to go home now," Kendra said.

Lesko looked over at Hubbs. The scientist's face was completely blank, his shoulders slumped. "Are you?" Lesko said pointlessly. "All right. Good. I mean it's good that you want to go home but—"

"I'll send a message," Hubbs said, saving him. Lesko could not tell if it was deliberate or if Hubbs was simply being himself. Did he see what was going on here? "Someone can come by to get you tomorrow, take you out of the desert if that is convenient."

"They killed my horse," she said dully.

"All right," Hubbs said after a moment. "I'll put the call in." His eyes were very nervous. "It would be best if you left here as quickly as possible; I agree with that." He reached toward the microphone.

"They had no right to kill my horse," Kendra said. "My grandfather was stupid, but at least it was his own choice. My grandmother too, and Clete. But my horse had nothing to say about it."

She reached toward the shelf above Hubbs, suddenly seized a vial, and raised it above her head. The glass twinkled in the fluorescence. Then she threw the vial to the floor, shattering it.

Hubbs and Lesko moved together, acting as a team for perhaps the first time. Ants, three of them, had rippled out on the floor, scurrying blindly for shelter, gelatinous fluid pouring from their bodies. Hubbs reached out and scooped them off the floor, careless of his safety, and as Lesko held out the vial, he inserted them, wriggling, one by one, into the open neck; then Lesko stoppered the vial and put it back on the rack. Hubbs, his face suffused with rage, stood to check the tracer mechanism; the ants had displaced it and it had ceased its printout. Lesko went to Kendra, pinned her arms carefully but harshly behind her back, and pulled her from the room, twisting them, giving enough pressure to force cooperation. She screamed then, the first sound in the room since the shattering of the vial. "You killed my horse!" she was saying. "You killed everyone!" But Lesko had her under control; he brought her all the way down the corridor and shoved her into an aseptic cubicle, the end of which was her room, and then he bolted the door and came back to the laboratory.

His feelings were a complex blend of fury and sympathy, but he guessed that fury predominated. Hubbs was right. The work had to go forward; nothing could stop them from that primary obligation, because only the work had reality, only the work had meaning . . . and if Hubbs were not able to continue his experiments, then they might indeed literally never get out of here. The ants were not fooling. There was nothing remotely comic about the situation. Yet, and he had to concede this, the girl was reacting normally . . . Hubbs and he were now so far from normal behavior that they were able to go forward with field studies in the aftermath of a tragedy that would have shattered, should have shattered, anyone in a normal condition; we are becoming monsters, Lesko thought, we are becoming the enemy, a wriggling mass of stimulus-response, and he went back into the laboratory, where he saw Hubbs, stunned, looking at the console, his body motionless. Above him, the ants and mantises moved within their separate vials. Hubbs's eyes were deep and stricken. He turned toward Lesko and showed him his wrist. Near the major vein was a deep imprint where his thumb had pressed, but that was not what he was showing nor what Lesko saw. Lesko looked at the small red mark and its spreading corona of stain.

"You've been bitten," Lesko said.

XII

The yellow poison had shocked them. The ants could not feel pain, but they could sense their losses with the dull precision with which a building might note the loss of its foundation and crumple, and now, their troops decimated, the queens, solemn in their chambers, could feel what had happened and every implication of it. The enemy was cunning and clever; their deadly compound had struck at the heart of the troops, and the queens in their dead way felt every loss. Soldiers, those that had not been exposed to the chemical, hovered around the queens, protecting them. The queens, without thought or language, meditated.

Something happened within the queens. A compound shifted, became something else; something too complex to be notated in chemical formulae occurred deep within the bodies. Yellow was absorbed, transversed through the devious interstices of the queens, and it muddled, changed colors, began to flow openly.

It flowed then like a river bursting free past an obstruction, the color shifting in the darkness of the interstices, first yellow, then something not yellow: red, green, purple, off-white, a chiaroscuro of colors, and then from the bodies of the queens, one by one, drifted eggs that were of a different color, and from those eggs came things—

—Came and came again, small, winged things, blind and yet cunning in the deep caves, scuttling in the ruined towers, and then pouring from them, moving irresistibly into the yellow streaks and fumes that persisted and—

—Moved beyond them, flowing over in waves, more eggs streaming out, hundreds in sequence now, the little black things pouring free and they dove, stalked, scuttled through the yellow untouched—

—By it, invulnerable, pouring out into the desert, their small soundless cries breaking into the coma of the queens, and the queens cried back, all of them in pulses of light and heat, a tight web of communication building and then flowering in the desert and then—

—The queens produced a shower of eggs, coming out in a clotted, unending outpour, light and heat making celebration in the desert.

Far away, another receptor twitched a signal it noted as *clear*.

PHASE III

Hubbs put a bandage on the place where he had been bitten and went on working with the computer. No time to waste. The small, red spot sealed off, drained imperceptibly. He said that it felt all right. In a pool of light, Hubbs sat at the keyboard attached to one of the computer banks.

He typed out symbols on a keyboard, waited. Something came back at him. The roller moved. Hubbs smiled with pleasure and looked at Lesko. His eyes were very bright.

"It's rather a crude language," he said. "But it's clear."

"Yes," Lesko said. He was at the next computer unit, for the first time in days totally absorbed in his work. Hubbs was right: the things were communicating, receiving messages, feeding them back. Simple commands produced clear patterns on the printout. "If I keep building up my library of sound words," he said, "I might actually strike up a conversation with them. Like the whales." He brushed sweat from his forehead. Kendra was somewhere at the back of his consciousness, but he was not really thinking of her now. Later. He would deal with that problem later; now there was work.

"Of course," he said, looking at the things in the vials, "we're talking about just a few survivors. The ants would have to come back . . . and we'd have to be here for a while."

"Indeed," Hubbs said.

"When is the helicopter coming, anyway?"

"It'll be here," Hubbs said. He put his fingers on the bandage, then ran them delicately up his arm. The spot was spreading little tendrils, fibers moving toward the arm crease.

"I'm sorry about that," he said.

"It's not your fault."

"We've got to get that treated."

"In time," Hubbs said, still looking at the infection. "I don't feel any pain. Insect bites are rarely serious."

"Ants are rarely serious, but these appear to be. I think we should have it looked at," Lesko said. "The 'copter is coming in for the girl I think that they should pick you up too and take you back to the base."

"And leave you here alone?" Hubbs said with a difficult attempt at a smile. "Just when we're on the verge of a significant breakthrough, and the invading hordes have been beaten back. Leave you to take all of the tributes from a grateful government?"

"That's ridiculous," Lesko said angrily. "For God's sake, you don't think that matters to me, do you? Besides, I'll take the 'copter back with you."

Hubbs said gently, "I was making an attempt at

humor, James. People like me really don't know how though, do we?" He rubbed the area again, wincing. "Besides, there's not enough room in one of these 'copters for three passengers. Even one is pushing it when you're flying against one of those winds. No, I'm going to stay here."

"I'll go back with you."

"And leave the girl here? No," Hubbs said. "I thought I told you, that's completely impossible. We came together, and we're going to finish this project the same way. I'm perfectly all right, I really am; and even if I'm not, if they've malevolently injected some slow-acting poison into my system, the deterioration seems to be so slow that I could be back in California, accepting a telephone call from the President before toxemia sets in." He looked at Lesko's blank face. "I'm trying a joke again, James," he said. "But I guess I'd better try no more."

"All right," Lesko said, vaguely embarrassed. Hubbs seemed more accessible and understandable to him by the moment; that was part of the trouble. He did not really like the man, probably never would, but more and more he saw his point. Kendra could have wrecked the project for them if they had not already arrived at the solution . . . he went back to the console, looked at the tracings.

"I don't have the faintest idea what they mean," he said. "But aren't they beautiful?"

"Yes," Hubbs said, looking over at the delicate tracings, weaving in patterns made through the stylus, geometric shapes, hexagons, pentagons, strangely exact and yet free-flowing . . . and all from the little figures in the tube. It was a mystery. "They're very beautiful. We're dealing with a kind of consciousness here, James, that is entirely different from ours . . .

77

and may be superior. The gestalt is a wholly acceptable means of alternative evolution, you know. It might have gone the other way entirely if our ancestors had not been so vicious. . . ."

His expression changed; he grabbed at his arm with pain, his mouth momentarily distorted.

Lesko stared at him.

II

Lesko's Diary: By the next morning, I knew that the situation had irrevocably changed, was no longer proceeding, could not proceed along predictable patterns. The ants had been destroyed by the insecticide; Hubbs had the situation seemingly under control; it was now only a matter of working out the communication patterns for future research . . . in short, on the face of the matter, all was over but the mopping up. But I knew that this was not so. I awoke with that peculiar and rather desperate apperception of doom that people who claim to have ESP state they have felt . . . to find out later that relatives have died, ships have been lost at sea, the mortgage application has fallen through, or similar disasters have occurred. The day as it progressed was a confirmation.

How is it possible to explain something like this? How can one communicate, particularly when one is a scientist supposedly dedicated to methodology, empiricism, the Socratic rule . . . how can one explain a totally unscientific and unempiric overlay of disasters that began with the dawn's early light and increased through all the moments of the morning, finally finding the most dreadful of confirmations? I can see that if I were able to give such explanation this would no longer be a scientific journal—which I still maintain is its purpose and its truest form—but one of those rather hysterical confessions associated with middle-aged women or middle-aged novels, small burblings of doom and discomfort while surrounded by neutral stimuli. How to explain that I awoke at seven in the morning stiff in the joints and with the feeling that all had been lost, that the success of the insecticide had been at best a temporary measure as the enemy regrouped, and that from this point onward the total disaster was beginning? Better not to explain this; I can see that I wax and wane upon abstraction; abstraction is at the center of these notes like a small, livid, beating heart, and it would be better to deal only with the objective facts of the matter as they correlate with my own reactions to them: i.e., empiricism and the scientific method. I will do my best. I will do the best that I can. Originally, I thought that these notes would find publication as a scientific abstract, but now I see that I will be quite lucky if I can place them in a confession magazine. More and more I am lurching out of control, deserting objectivity for neurasthenia. It may be that the ants, or what remains of them, are sending out mysterious deathly rays (I feel that this should be capitalized: Mysterious Deathly Rays) to destroy my mind and abort my conscious, but then again what I may truly need is a long rest that I can obtain upon the completion of this project. We will see. I do not know if this project has a completion. I am not sure of anything anymore, which is a poor position for a scientist.

I awoke from a jagged sleep that had been filled with images of ants, smashed towers, broken mounds, surges of power from the towers, and scurrying ants sent by the towers to attack, only to find the station deadly quiet, the low hum of the computer washing it with gentle sound. Outside, the desert was littered with little bodies of all colors: as far as I could see, dead and poisoned ants lay upon the beach of desert like snowflakes. The yellow had lifted during the night as the P-2 was absorbed by the atmosphere or vice versa and had now become a spectrum of colors ranging from deep violet through clear white, a thin haze of vapors rising into the sunlight. The ruined truck was now clearly visible only fifty or sixty yards downrange. Darkness creates a different perception of distance and time; staggering with Kendra back from the accident last night, it had felt like miles, but all of this, three deaths, the attack, and the destruction of the ants, had occurred within a short distance of the station. We thought, dear Lord, that we were operating on a cosmic scale, and all the time it was happening in some clotheshamper of possibility.

Donning my humble scientific garb, I left my cubicle, walked down the hallway, peeked into Hubbs's quarters (no larger than mine; the democratic principle), which were vacant, indicating either that he had persisted with his infernal experiments all night long or more likely had risen early to resume them. I thought of going into the laboratory to check on him—that had been, after all, a nasty welt on his arm: I agreed with him in doubting that it was truly dangerous, but the mysteriousness of the ants made every wound inflicted by them equally mysterious; *I* would not have wanted to carry around that bite, much less be working with it. I went into Kendra's quarters, deciding that I had world enough and time to deal with Hubbs, and our relations were deteriorating so rapidly anyway that it was not necessary to force the issue. Also, I badly wanted to see Kendra.

I do not deny it; the girl has affected (or afflicted) me deeply. My dreams in part had been occupied with images of Kendra superimposed against a struggling mass of ants, her face translucent so that a clear pattern of ants could be seen wriggling behind her, but somehow she was indefinably sad, having an opacity of expression that matched the translucence of her flesh so that she was still and always herself. My tenuous relations with women seemed to have already reached a complete ambiguity with Kendra. Carrying her back to the station, the softness of her body against mine, I had succumbed to a series of images of Kendra naked, Kendra reaching, Kendra groaning out her need . . . and those images, rather than giving me appeasement, had made me only more uncomfortable, converted my walk into a stumble, and I had been even more anxious than Hubbs to drop her in her room and return to our experiments . . . a mistake the more tragic because of her nearly successful attempt to destroy our experimental subjects. Hubbs, when she had smashed the vial, had had a look of murder, but my own feelings were too amorphous to be easily understood. Perhaps I admired her for that. I wish that I could smash these experiments with the same dispatch that she summoned because ultimately I feel that we are involved in something very wrong here, that there are mysteries we cannot penetrate, that our apparent vanquishing of the ants has been merely a matter of gaining time . . . and that we

would be well-advised to clamber aboard that helicopter when it comes and get out of here as quickly
as Kendra, and spread the warning to everyone that
serious things are happening/have happened out here
on the desert. Of course I will not do this. Who
would listen? What does the invasion of the ants matter to the urbanite on the eastern slab or for that
matter any resident of Tucson a scant two hundred
miles from here? No one would know; nobody cares.
Hubbs and I are going to stay to finish these experiments. Only he can give the order to leave.

I went to her room and found her sleeping, but
smiling in her sleep in so fresh and open a way that I
could have grasped her for sheer pity, her brown
hair tossing on the pillow, her lovely bare arms extended as if in greeting to something unknown behind
the sheet of her eyelids, and then, all in a tumble
but still graceful (how many of us can do this gracefully?), she awakened, sitting bolt upright in the bed,
shaking her head, looking at me. First her eyes were
panels of fear and then they softened, moistened toward something else. The circumstances of her presence filtered into her and her face became closed over
although still lovely. She looked at and then away
from me as if I were somehow responsible for her being here.

"Hey," I said to her. I went to the foot of the cot
and kneeled there, looking at her as a zoo creature
might look at some novel and beautiful wild thing.
"Do you remember me?" I said to her quietly, using
my voice to pace her slowly from sleep. "Surely you
remember me."

She nodded, slowly. "Yes," she said. "I do."
"You're a wonderful sleeper."
Her eyes rimmed, her mouth twiched in panic.

"Did I oversleep?" she said. She put a leg out of the cot. "Oh, my God, I hope—"

"No," I said, taking her arm. Soft and white, it fell into my palm like a bow in a hunter's hand. "No, no, I was just making a little joke." She fluttered against me. I felt like Hubbs; trying to connect in a language I did not understand, and did not know. "Take it easy," I said intensely, and through force of pressure if not belief, I felt her relax slightly. "Please relax; it's important." She collapsed then, lying on the cold metal rack of the bed as if that act was a sacrament.

"How are you feeling?" I asked after a while, realizing that I had been staring at her without words for quite a time and that she had received that gaze unmoving, unoffended. A signal? Or merely her fear. Certainly, Hubbs and I must have been terrifying to her.

"I'm better," she said. "I guess I'll be all right." Her eyes wandered. "Maybe."

"You will be."

"How is—" she said and then stopped. I thought that she was unable to utter his name for hatred and then realized, feeling foolish, that she simply did not remember it. Or mine either.

"Hubbs," I said. "Dr. Ernest Hubbs. He's all right. He'll survive."

"Good."

"My name is James Lesko. You can call me Jim."

She thought about it. "All right, Jim," she said, and then after a time, "I lied when I said it was good that Dr. Hubbs would survive. Actually, I'm really sorry to hear that."

"Taste is taste," I said and shrugged. In a hideous way, I realized, we were making what is called small talk. One of the advantages of that alternative form of evolution Hubbs and I had discussed is that there would be no need for small talk in a subverbal society. What did the ants do to pass the time, then? Doubtless they worked. I was babbling internally throughout this stream of consciousness, but for some reason I felt happier than I had in days, anyway. The nearness. It must have been the nearness of her. Every popular song one hears contains a particular of truth. I could see that.

"If I were you, I would have done the same thing," I said. "I don't blame you for swinging out at them that way."

"Oh?"

"You have a mean swing."

"Thanks," she said. I realized that she did not know what I was talking about. She had no memory at all of last night. I decided to let it go.

"I'm afraid," she said, her expression changing. She looked nervously through the room, which fortunately had no windows, it having been designed that way. The station is a portable, sealed unit; the living quarters are cubes attached to the main bank.

"What's wrong?" I said pointlessly.

"My grandparents are dead. Aren't they?"

"Yes they are."

"And Clete. Clete is dead too."

"Yes he is," I said. I nodded, said slowly, "All of them are dead. You're lucky to have survived. You were younger than they and stronger or it would have been you too." I let her think about that for a while and said, "They were old people. They wouldn't have lived much longer anyway. You have your whole life in front of you; you couldn't have stayed with them in the desert."

"Yes I could."

"All right," I said. "Have it your way. You could have. Don't you have any parents?"

"I have no one," she said. "No one at all."

"Neither do I," I said. The way it came out I sounded almost cheerful, and this slash of morbidity —feeling that I could become closer to her because of the deaths, that is—was so sickening that for a moment I could not bear myself. "You must be hungry," I said, a reasonable way of changing the subject. "How about having some breakfast?"

"All right," she said. She put her feet on the floor, came slowly but gracefully out of bed. Standing, she was closer to my height than I had realized, five seven or eight perhaps, and she carried herself with a dignity and grace that few women have. "Let's go," she said.

"Into the galley," I said. I put out a hand instinctively, without even thinking about it, and she took it delicately. I led her from the room down a long hallway, equipment hanging from the ceiling in clumps like flowers: the wiring and network having the aspect of foliage. We could have been in a jungle, although, of course, we were not.

"Can I ask you a question?" she said, stopping. I drew up gently, feeling her palm against mine. It would be partially inaccurate to say that simply holding her hand aroused me (and would make me appear some kind of a sexual lunatic as well), but I felt something very much like arousal, I would concede this. Call it an excess of tenderness.

"By all means," I said.

"What exactly are you doing here?"

"We're doing a little research into statistical probabilities," I said.

"Does it have to do with the ants?"

"I should say so," I said. "I would say that the

coefficient of correlation between the presence of ants and our own presence is close to point ninety . . . as you may be well aware."

"No," she said. "You don't understand me. I know you're here about the ants, the two of you that is. And he's the one who killed my grandparents and Clete with his insecticide. But what do *you* do?"

"I'm the statistical part of the team," I said. "He performs the experiments and I record them. He does the killing and I do the body count. Like that. Do you understand?"

She looked at me blankly. "I think so," she said.

"Statisticians are famous for their peculiar relationship to fact. They both do and do not participate. But I want to be perfectly fair about this," I said judiciously. "Firing off the insecticide might have been his idea, but I hardly protested. In fact I cooperated willingly. The only thing I wouldn't have done was to attack the towers."

She started to walk again, pushing me gently. "I don't think I understand a word you're saying," she said.

"That's perfectly all right. Most people don't."

"But I guess that your work must be very interesting."

"Oh, it is," I said, leading her into the galley. "It's fascinating." There was barely enough space for the two of us in the little enclosure, but I only found the compression gratifying. Shoulder to shoulder with her, I opened a rack above and showed her the menu. "Powdered milk, powdered juice, powdered eggs, dehydrated bacon," I said. "Just like home. But then again, what's so great about home?"

"Are you in there, James?" Hubbs said from somewhere. We both jumped. "Come in here as soon as you're finished, please. There are some things I want to show you."

Kendra's face was blank. "I'd better go," I said.

"All right."

"You can make yourself something."

"If you say so."

"Are you okay?" I said. I was propelled by something that I thought was anxiety but which I now understand was only a reluctance to leave her. I did not want to leave her. "If you're not—"

She nodded. "I'm all right," she said. "Why don't you make yourself something to eat?"

"I'm not hungry."

"James," Hubbs said again. "We've got problems here; I'm afraid that you'd better come as soon as you can."

She held that curious, intense look on me. "You're afraid of him, aren't you?" she said.

"Not exactly. But I am his assistant."

"All right," she said. "You're not afraid of him."

There was nothing else to say. She still looked at me levelly; she would have held that position indefinitely. I touched her on the shoulder gently and worked my way past her. Is it possible that I *am* afraid of Hubbs? The thought had never previously occurred to me, and it seems on the face of it to be ridiculous; we have the normal superior/assistant relationship, but I had never equated cooperation with fear. They are two entirely different things. Still, it is something worth considering. Is it possible that I have been intimidated all my life; that instinctively I place myself in a position of dependence to everyone with whom I work? Is it possible, for that matter, that I went into game theory simply because it gave me the illusion of control in a universe where even random factors would be plotted? All of these are chilling thoughts that may force me to rethink a number of assumptions, but there has simply been no time yet for such reflection, events overtaking us as they have. Still, it is interesting and frightening material. Do I identify with the ants, am I so immersed in this project now because unlike the products of individuating evolution the ants have neither a superior nor inferior relation to any of their fellows? Does the gestalt fascinate me because a gestalt by definition makes no demands upon the discrete individual parts, enables them to flow into the overall pattern? I do not know. I simply do not know.

I left Kendra and went into the laboratory.

III

That unnatural brightness was flaring deep into Hubbs's eyes, and he had contrived to wear his jacket in such a way that it completely obscured his arm from wrist to shoulder. "Look, James," he said as Lesko came in, motioning with the unwounded arm through the window. "I may be entirely wrong about this, but we seem to be under a state of siege."

Lesko's gaze followed Hubbs's arm. Outside in the sand, two small mounds about the size of a man's head were pulsating on the desert. They were the color of mud, appeared to be at least partially liquefied, and it seemed to Lesko that there was an antlike expression on each of them . . . they seemed to hint at ants' faces. Behind them, the gutted towers stood, their color now a dead white.

"Well, what the hell is that?" Lesko said.

"Well," Hubbs said cheerfully, "it's no optical illusion, my boy. It's more than reflected sunlight. Our interior temperature is already up more than five degrees."

"Good Lord," Lesko said and noticed for the first time that it was indeed warm in the laboratory, warmer than it had ever been before. He verified this with a quick look at the wall thermometer, feeling sweat suddenly pool in his armpits.

"And there's another interesting detail as well," Hubbs said, motioning toward the mounds again. "How do you suppose the ants were able to build on a poison strip where they absolutely cannot live?" He struggled one-handed with the computer controls, his face flushed. "Think about that," he said.

"Did you say five degrees?"

"Five degrees in an hour and a half," Hubbs said. "I've been sitting here and watching it, and it's been very interesting, let me tell you. It's fascinating to watch a thermometer inch its way up when it's really measuring your survival. The sun is far from full strength, of course; I don't think we've begun to see what we will. Now watch this."

Lesko stared as Hubbs worked the controls of the television monitor. Now Lesko could see a close-up of the mounds outside, the remote camera closing in; the mounds under inspection were not solid but intersticed, a collection of channels in a network that seemed to be more open than closed, a dull whirring aspect of inner light that reminded Lesko of the look of the galaxies in a slide show. "Did you say five degrees?" Lesko said, putting a finger inside his collar and pushing it away gently. It was definitely a nervous reaction, he thought, and yet it seemed definably hotter. He was sweating.

"This is fascinating," Hubbs said. "Just watch the monitors, pay some attention for once in your life to something actually going on." His tone was bantering not harsh. "You know," he said, "if there weren't lives at stake here, if those filthy little buggers weren't actual murderers, I suppose one could see beauty in this. Wouldn't you agree?"

The camera tracked in, picking up movement as programmed, and a single ant burst into focus. Lesko, fascinated now, watched it bobble in front of the camera. It was almost as if it were bowing, pleased with its new role as a star of stage and screen. Then the camera tracked in to the underbelly, and Lesko's eyes widened.

The ant, below all of its cilia, was yellow.

He turned to Hubbs, his fingers scrappling at the shelf where momentarily he had to support himself. "My God," he said. "It's—"

"Yellow," Hubbs said helpfully. "It's quite yellow."

"It's apparently integrated—"

Hubbs had had more time to think about this. His voice was calm and soothing, although, Lesko thought, slightly mad. "Isn't it a beautiful adaptation?" he said. "They are absolutely fantastic. We challenge and they respond. They're most attentive."

More ants appeared in the picture, scuttling, rounding the first who reared on his hind legs as if distressed to share any part of the camera. Then, instinct predominating, it joined the gathering mass and they marched off. They looked quite intent and busy. Happy ants. Well-oriented into their subculture. Highly motivated and flourishing with stimulus-response. No anomie for them, Lesko thought, and wondered if he was giggling; no, these ants were psychically in excellent condition. There seemed to be no lag between their efforts and their goals, their intentions and their activities. The genius of the gestalt. The superiority of parallel evolution. Lesko found that he was breathing through his mouth, gasping, really; he closed it and turned away, went to the window, and looked at the sands of the desert, more innocent without remote magnification.

"We're going to fry in here," he said.

"You know what my question is?" Hubbs said, turning from the monitor, which now showed an abcess no less empty than what Lesko saw through the window. "I have a very simple question. What do they want? What are their goals?" His eyes gleamed; he wiped sweat from his forehead and inspected it. "They definitely are after something."

Lesko's control snapped. It went suddenly, like a rubber band overextended. "They have no goals!" he said loudly. "Now stop personalizing them. And you ought to get that bite looked at."

"Now you're wrong," Hubbs said quietly. "You're just not looking at the realities of this, James. You saw how they disabled that truck and killed those unfortunate people. And now this—"

"Listen to me," Lesko said with growing anger; he turned from the window, his voice rising to a shout, "I came here to do three weeks of science in the sun. To assist you in trying to establish some interconnection with ants that are neither malevolent nor benevolent but simply appear to be a mutated species doing antlike things in a more than antlike way. All

91

right? I did not sign up for a goddamned war against a bunch of goddamned ants, and what the hell did you shoot off the top of those towers for? Why? *Why?*" His throat was hoarse; he coughed, hawked, spat to the side, and rubbed the spittle into dryness. Hubbs watched him quietly, not moving. After a little while, Lesko felt his rage pass as quickly as it had come. "I repeat," he said in his most reasonable voice, "why *did* you destroy the towers?"

"Bait."

"Bait?" Lesko said, stunned. "What are you—"

"Well, look here now," Hubbs said, and Lesko made his final decision right then: the man *was* mad; he had been uncertain about it for a while, but no longer. It was entirely clear. "Look here, I had to get them to attack. Didn't I? They're rather intelligent you know. I thought you observed the geometric pattern in the field. What have you been doing if you haven't picked up on that by now?"

"You saw intelligence?" Lesko said quietly.

"Of couse I saw it."

"What does intelligence have to do with any of it? There are dead people—"

"Intelligence," Hubbs says, "is the key to design, my boy. Once we realize that we are dealing with an intelligence equal to ours, if entirely different in origin and function, we are trembling on the verge of the truly significant. It is no longer, as you put it, three weeks of research in the sun, but possibly the most important project in the history of the National Science Institute. Or don't you know that?"

"I don't know anything now. I'm shocked," Lesko said. "I'm shocked and I'm getting sick and the temperature is rising—"

Hubbs looked at him, saying nothing. For a little

while, Lesko did not know what the man's expression was, then it came to him. Of course. Hubbs was crazy, and his look was a look of triumph.

"Why didn't you say something?" he said. "If you were so impressed by their intelligence and the rising significance—"

"Why didn't you?" Hubbs said. "You knew it, didn't you? You know those are no ordinary ants we're dealing with, that we've got a malevolent, active intelligence on our hands out there, one whose evolutionary process can instantly adapt to survival and counterattack. Don't deny it, James! You know that's exactly what we have!"

"All right," Lesko said. "I knew it." He felt as if he was staggering through one of those idiotic obligatory scenes at the end of a dramatic second act when characters talk to one another ponderously, wrapping up all the things that they have been doing since the rise of curtain. Making things easier for the audience. But this was displacement, he thought, feeling sick; he was trying to think of this as a play and his conversation with Hubbs as a second act curtain, but outside there were real ants on a real desert . . . and they were out to kill them. "I didn't even want to discuss it with you," he said. "You weren't interested in their intelligence! All you wanted to do was to kill them, and now you've given them the message."

"You should have talked it over with me," Hubbs said. "We should have talked it over with one another. We knew what we had, didn't we? But nobody wanted to talk. I was very much afraid that you'd be terrified and run away, and I needed you."

"To go out into the desert," Lesko said and nodded. "To go out into the desert and check out some dead people, that's what you needed me for.

Well, the hell with all of that. When is the goddamned helicopter coming."

Hubbs stood there. Lesko caught up in the intensity
of their dialogue, only noticed now that Hubbs was
standing in a strange, cramped position; his injured
arm shoved deep into his pocket, concealed by the
jacket. Under the pale skin, the network radiating
from the bite seemed to be spreading up into his
face. . . .

"James," Hubbs said earnestly. "Don't you see?
We are faced with a power that has appeared almost
spontaneously and that is now exerting itself. We have
the opportunity to study it, to learn from it, to teach
it its limitations. We can, in a word, educate it."

Lesko stared at Hubbs; then his gaze tracked back
to the monitor, which, the ants having disappeared, had
returned to the two mounds on the desert. They shone
like eyes against the reflected sun. "You said you
called the helicopter," he said quietly, trying to talk
smoothly.

"We could use another variety of insecticide,"
Hubbs said. "But they would only adapt again, probably more quickly this time. Acceleration. So we
must consider other alternatives."

Lesko felt as if he were losing his sense of balance,
but it would be, unfortunately, only a neurasthenic
reaction again. He would never be so fortunate as to
simply collapse and be out of this situation. "You
mean?" he said quietly, getting out every word as if
it were a discovery of language, "that you didn't call
for the helicopter?"

"You see," Hubbs said conversationally, looking
past him, "it is vital that they have the opportunity
to test their power against ours . . . and learn from

94

the consequences. We must teach them a lesson that the filthy little bastards will never forget."

"Hubbs," Lesko said, moving toward the door, "I'm going to call in. I'm going to call in and tell them not only to take the girl and myself out of here, I'm going to tell them to take you out too."

"You won't call," Hubbs said as Lesko flung open the door and walked down the small corridor to the communications room, looking for the radio. Of course Hubbs would have hidden the microphone. He was not even going to waste time looking for it. "You won't call," Hubbs was saying, "because you are as fascinated by the challenge of this mission as I am. Don't deny it. You love science, Lesko; you've become an ascetic just like myself, cut yourself off from much human contact, denied the vagrant impulses of what we ascetics call the flesh, just so that you could be immersed more deeply—"

"Go to hell!" Lesko screamed and picked up the auxiliary microphone wired into the radio and flipped the contact switch. A violent spark rimmed the console, leaping from the shielded wires against the steel surfaces, and then, almost anticlimactically, there was a crackle and like something exhaled from the lungs of a cigarette smoker a lazy puff of smoke darted across the room, and landed like a fish against the wall, shattering.

"You son of a bitch," Lesko said.

He reached under the radio for the emergency kit, found the power tool and put on the switch. This one worked. Desperately, careless of the damage the heat was inflicting on his palms, he sawed at the shielding and opened up the radio like a walnut, staring at the blackened metal and wires. Then he shut off the saw, dropped it to the floor beside him, and rubbed his palms slowly, feeling the little scales of the burn already emerging.

"Dirty bastards," he said. Then something in the wiring attracted him and he looked more closely, bending over.

Two yellow-bellied ants lay in the wiring. They had, of course, been electrocuted, but all in all, Lesko decided, staring at them, they had probably died happy. They had not even died at all.

He turned toward Hubbs. "You know what has happened?" he said.

"I know."

"We're cut off!"

"I know," Hubbs said again. "I know that very well, and I'm glad. Because it's going to make our success now all the sweeter."

Hubbs extended his injured hand in a gesture, momentarily forgetful. Lesko saw the enlargement then, the hand bright red and dangling off the wrist, literally inflated with blood, the huge, mangled hand of the insect bite—

Hubbs, seeing Lesko's face, gasped with realization and hid the hand awkwardly behind his back.

Lesko kept on staring at him, and after a moment, with a series of whimpering and embarrassed little murmurs, Hubbs went back to the console.

IV

Lesko's Diary: So we were sealed in, cut off from the world. Oddly, this realization did not lift me toward panic, but did the reverse. It put a cap on the frantic emotions that had begun to spill over during the talk with Hubbs, my realization that he was mad, my further realization that the situation was far more serious than either of us (and I will share the blame here) had wanted to admit.

It was that kind of confirmation of utter disaster that enables people to get through crises; the dying relatives, the out-of-control car, the diving airplane, all of those things that finally confirm that suspicion, we are born with and drag around like baggage through all of our days . . . that we are mortal creatures poised in a frail fashion on the rim of the earth; that we are dying, that we will die, that we are already dead, that our undoing is carried within us in the very message of the cells, the rising of the blood as it pounds through the distended heart a million times a day . . . and knowing this, knowing that we are doomed, we tend to draw strength from extrinsic confirmation of this, rather than succumb to weakness. Well, we always knew it, it is possible to say, looking at the father dying of cancer. Ah, well, no one lives forever, as the car, completely out of control, speeds toward an abutment, the tires and brakes and steering quite gone; oh, well, it could have been worse, it might have happened years ago, we repeat, as the plane soars and then falls toward the earth at a mile and a half a second. It is a reversion to paganism, of course, but it is not the paganism that will kill us as much as the insulating effects of a civilization that progressively will not allow us true contact and meaningful acknowledgment of our terrors. Is this not true, gentlemen of the scientific jury? Of course it is true; all of you know in your deadly and shriveled hearts that I speak nothing but the truth . . . apologies for this lecture, of course.

Hubbs went back to the computer bank, the monitor; I followed him. There was nothing else to do. We were in for it now, all right, and I felt a peculiar and dismal sense of exaltation for reasons that I have explained above, quite satisfactorily I am sure. Exaltation pursued me into that room, threw a little shroud around my shoulders, and, although I shrugged it off, it stayed with me a bit; I went through the next moments in a peculiar glow of ebullience. Like Hubbs, I was no longer, in the strictest sense of the word, quite sane. Still, who is? Are you, gentlemen? I looked at the thermometer for the first time.

The thermometer had two sides; one linked into the computer to show its interior temperature, the other refracting our own, somewhat humbler atmosphere. It showed that the temperature in our humble station was ninety-one degrees; bad enough for a man with an ant bite, I would think, but more ominously the computer temperature was eighty-six. That creature of temperate clime, the computer, muttered and mumbled to itself. Hubbs, having readjusted his clothing to once again conceal the deformity of his hand, a contrived casualness in the way the jacket, slung over his shoulder, managed to conceal any sight of the wound, stood by the computer like an overprotective parent, his uninjured hand on the shielding. He looked at me quite pleasantly as I came in, trying to make amends, I suppose, for the personality conflicts exposed by our conversation, feeling a little guilty about the failure to call the helicopter as promised. On the other hand, and this thought has just occurred to me, his pleasant bearing may have come out of no impulse whatsoever to make amends . . . it may simply have been that Hubbs did not even remember our conversation, his mind being long gone into other matters. This is possible; for one thing, I had completely forgotten Kendra's presence in the galley, and if it was possible for me to forget her, Hubbs could certainly let a small detail like our conversation slip by.

"When does the computer kick off?" he asked quite levelly.

"Don't you know?"

"Tell me," he said. His tone was quite reasonable, modulated, and pleasantly controlled. If nothing else, the ant bite had done wonders for his manner; this new Hubbs was far less pedantic.

I looked at the thermometer, which had now moved up to the small line separating degree marks. "Coming up to eighty-seven. It kicks off at ninety," I said.

"Ninety, huh?"

"That's according to the manual," I said. "But who knows? Maybe ninety-one. Maybe eighty-nine. I don't know the exact tolerance levels of this machine."

"Well," Hubbs said cheerfully. "I believe that we're going to have a very spirited and even contest, James."

99

I looked up at him. "You're out of your mind," I said.

He reacted to this as if I had told him that he had a small spot on his nose. Not at all disconcerted, he rubbed at the bridge with his uninjured hand, then dropped it. "No I'm not," he said. "I'm perfectly sane, James, and so are you. We are dealing with a cunning enemy whose methods of thought and processes of action are entirely different from ours, and to a degree, as is common in modern psychological warfare, I've had to adopt their way of thinking so that I can anticipate them. That's all."

"I don't see the point in more destruction," I said. For the first time that morning, I looked at the ruined towers. They were just barely visible from this angle. The off-white, dead color had remained, but in some imperceptible way, they seemed to be changing. A look of implosion, crumbling-inward, that kind of thing.

"You have a serious misconception of what we're doing," Hubbs said. "Our goal is *not* destruction. This is not a military operation. We are not, per se, trying to eliminate the ants."

"We're not?"

"No."

Hubbs looked up at me then, his eyes quite clear, and he seemed to give me a wink. "That might have been my original intention, but I am no longer interested in destroying them," he said quietly. "Rather, our goal is in the conditioning of an intelligence that is as yet not goal-directed, that can be—"

His expression changed. He fluttered against the wall like a butterfly. "Get her out of here," he said thickly. "Get her out!"

I turned. Kendra had come into the laboratory, was

standing docilely at the door. I had become so absorbed in my discussion with Hubbs, so shocked by my rising and disastrous insight into the man that I had literally, as I have already said, forgotten her. For a moment, it was like looking at a stranger; I had to study her to remember who she was, and then everything came flooding back. Stimulus: response. The ant intelligence must have worked in that fashion, triggered by various extrinsic stimuli. *We were turning into ants ourselves.* "Get her out of here," Hubbs said again.

"No," I said. "She's going to stay."

Kendra walked cautiously over to the shelves, stared at the equipment on them. She made no move to seize anything. Hubbs smiled awkwardly. "I can't argue with you, James," he said. "If it comes to a question of sheer, physical force you can, of course, get your way. Only the will is important, that and the work. All right. Let her stay."

"You didn't want her out," I said reasonably enough. "You could have called the helicopter, but you didn't. So you obviously want her here. She can't be any more dangerous to us than the ants."

Hubbs thought about this for a while. "In other words," he said, "she is part of the circumstances of the challenge."

"Exactly. Why not?"

"Why not indeed? All right," he said almost cheerfully, going over to the air-conditioning unit. "The temperature is now up to eighty-seven. I will reset the controls so that we may begin."

"Begin what?"

"Our experiments, of course," he said and began to fiddle with the controls. I walked over to Kendra, who was standing there quietly, hands folded in front of her in a posture of absolute submissiveness. She looked up and smiled at me, and I realized her helplessness to say nothing of my own feelings that had muddled rapidly from infatuation to a kind of protectiveness even more dangerous to both of us. I wanted to touch her, but this, of course, was unthinkable in front of Hubbs. I knew that the man was mad. The poison from the ant bite had probably worked its way all through his system. Still, mad or sane, the experiments would have to continue. Wouldn't they? Eventually, I thought, the base might get curious on its own and send out a 'copter. We were spending a good deal of money after all, and they had already generated much anxiety on that score. It might only be a few more minutes or hours with the crazed Hubbs, and then we would return to base together. At least this was how I had worked things out in my mind. It seemed a wonderful way of looking at the matter.

"Kendra," I said, feeling pedagogic, all the feeling rushing outside in an impulse to give her vast amounts of information. "Would you like to see what we're doing here?"

"Yes," she said uncertainly. She might as well have said *no*. I could understand her problem. Doubtless she had taken the two of us for insane; still, what was her alternative to staying here? She could hardly run screaming into the desert, and after what she had been through last night, the station might have been a haven for her.

"I'll show you," I said. "This is all very interesting. We're in a battle with some very intelligent and malevolent ants."

"Which," Hubbs burbled, struggling with the dials,

"we're going to win, of course, because our intelligence is far more sophisticated."

"Oh," she said. "Of course we'll win. With two people like you commanding the battle, how could we possibly lose?"

I looked at her.

Her eyes were shrouded.

V

Kendra watched while the two of them went through their next experiment. She assumed that it was an experiment, in any event, that was what they told her they were doing, and she was not going to argue with them. She was not going to argue with anyone anymore, least of all these two. She had come to the conclusion that they were insane. The younger one, Lesko, was attractive and was insane in a rather nice way, whereas Hubbs, the senior man, was simply crazed, but neither one of them was at all near sanity. But because she was locked up in this station with them, apparently without any hope of escape, she would have to cooperate with them. Humor. Humor them. Humor crazy people. She was pretty sure that this was the right tactic anywhere. She had read someplace that the best tactic with the insane was to go along with their obsessions, agree with what they were saying, not to oppose them in any way but rather try to enter their fantasies. She would try to do this. What were they after? What did these men want?

They wanted, she guessed, to destroy the ants. That was a reasonable thing for them to try to do; yet between the ants and Hubbs, there was no saying as to which was the more dangerous. The ants, she supposed. The ants would be. They had killed her grandparents and their hired men, had ravaged the desert, killed her horse, changed the entire context of her life . . . yes, indeed, the ants were dangerous. They had to be respected, and what was going on here was obviously not a game of any sort.

But these men were dangerous too. She knew that it was Hubbs who in a way had been responsible for all the deaths by firing at the towers. If he had left the towers alone, the ants would not have been maddened, they would not have attacked, and her grandparents and Clete would still be alive. But then again, if he had not attacked, the ants might simply have waited for a better time to launch their deadly little waves of attention. But then, still again, the ants might have been peaceable, might have been goaded to the attack by the poisoned gas . . . and if Lesko was supposed to be such a good man, why hadn't he stopped it? Why hadn't he stopped Hubbs?

No. He had not. Quite to the contrary, he was Hubbs's enthusiastic helper. He had seemed sympathetic this morning; for a few moments, she thought that there was actually feeling there, but then after she had eaten and seen him in the laboratory, all of that had gone away from him. All that he was was Hubbs's helper, and there had been no need to interpret the look on his face when she came into that laboratory. He had been so absorbed that for an instant he had not even known who she was. He had been involved in his ant experiments, working with Hubbs on another way to attack them. So . . . so much for Lesko. There was no help here, not from either of them. Nevertheless, she had to cooperate. Having accepted the fact that both of them were insane was perfectly all right, but did this do anything to get her out of this? No, it did not.

"White noise," Lesko was saying to her, his eyes very intense and bright. "What we're going to do is to throw every sound in the world at them." He jiggled dials on a console. A low hum filled the laboratory. Hubbs was working away in a corner on a roller of paper, making notes. The hum was unpleasant, grating; it cut in under her consciousness and made her nauseous. "I know," Lesko said, seeing her face. "It's quite upsetting, covering as it does the entire frequency belt. Now that noise, white noise I should say, is, is an amalgam of every noise in the world, from one end of that belt to the next." He twisted another dial, his fingers poised and delicate. "We're throwing it right into those mounds outside," he said, "which we assume to be the place to which the ant colony has transferred, at least the mobile sectors of it. We're throwing this noise, as I say, right down their throats on a series of frequencies, and do you know what's going to happen?"

"No," Kendra said. "I do not."

"Then let me tell you," Lesko said and put an arm around her shoulder. She felt the soaking pressure of his body; it sickened her and yet on another level created a vague excitement. "Now this white noise, which soaks up the entire range of amplitude, so to speak, is being beamed directly into them, and it's going to come back. Minus one crucial element of course."

"Of course," she said dully.

She looked out the windows, toward the mounds of which he was speaking. There they were, heaped like breasts on the desert. Instinctively, she touched her own. They felt full and hard, but it was not passion that had brought them up but something indefinable. He looked at her and self-conscious, embarrassed, she dropped her hands to her sides, curling them.

"Do you want to know what that element is?" he said awkwardly.

"If you want to tell me."

"You're not really interested," he said. "You're not really interested in any of this. You think that we're crazy."

"No, I don't," she said, looking away from the mounds. Hubbs was working feverishly on some sheets of paper in the corner, pausing now and then to swear and to inhale deeply. "I don't think you're crazy."

"It doesn't matter," Lesko said. "Crazy or sane, we're in a very serious situation. Don't you know that?"

"Now I do. Yes, I do."

"Do you know what my theory is?" Lesko said.

"You think that the ants want to take over the world," Kendra said. "You think that they're responding to some set of instructions from a higher power or something like that and that they're going to take over everything unless you and Dr. Hubbs stop them right here."

He stared at her and his hand went instinctively to his forehead.

"I know," she said. "I know exactly what you think. That's why Dr. Hubbs blew up the towers, isn't it? To attack them directly before they were able to get their forces together."

She stared at him levelly, and although she despised herself for this, felt a spark of triumph because she knew she was right. Of course she was right. She did not know a word of their science, but she knew what was in their murderous, maniacal hearts.

Unspeaking, he finally looked away from her.

VI

Lesko's Diary: The idea was to hurl white sound into them, pure noise; it would come back on the tracking channel lacking only that frequency on which they broadcast . . . and by doing this, we would know how they could be reached. With luck we could use the transmitter broadcasting that frequency to destroy their communication. But looking at Kendra, it suddenly seemed quite pointless: I do not refer only to the experiment but to the struggle itself, the totality of it. Why, after all, were we challenging the ants? What was the meaning of all of it? This slash of futility, so unexpected and so completely reasonable in the force with which it struck, unsettled me, made me literally stagger, and it was with an effort that I pulled my attention from Kendra and back to the board itself on which the flickering of light indicated that the transmitter was ready. But that one moment of *angst* during which, however briefly, the entire point of our struggles had looked meaningless stayed with me; I knew that in some deep sense I would never be the same person again maintaining the same attitudes. I say *angst* but this was not quite the feeling that ran through me; it is better to be honest in this journal and say that what happened was that I suddenly had a clear moment of anticipation, could look into the open shell of the future cleaving open like a walnut, and I said *that the ants were going to win* and nothing could be done about it. Hubbs in his obsession to do battle or die, Kendra in her ignorance, myself in my ambivalence, all of us were locked into our separate responses, but they were of equal futility because the ants had no responses at all nor did they have any range of feeling. Individuating evolution led to individuating reaction . . . but the ants had no such problem. One for all and all for one. We simply could not deal with this. The only question was what the ants wanted, because if they wanted our destruction, and this seemed likely, they would have it. Who were we fooling with our white noise, our grenades, our insecticides, our arguments? I thought. We certainly were not deceiving the ants, for they were as careless of our emotions as Hubbs had been of their towers when, with whatever futility, he had destroyed them.

I told Kendra to sit in a corner of the laboratory while we worked with the sound generator. Activity was best: while doing useful things, arranging an experiment, plotting out possibilities one could think that the campaign against the ants was going well, or at least that it was going. Feed in the tape, arrange the amplifiers, check the printouts, create the sound mix. Force lever B over lever A. Check out oscillation. Watch the frequency belt. Earnest scientific acts performed deftly and with style. The ants had no style or science, of course. They simply performed. If we had evolved in a different way, we would have been performers too. Instead, we had developed a society, a code, a technology that was itself merely an excuse for inaction.

Hubbs threw in the generator, his swollen red hand exposed, and the white noise began. Even though it was being thrown outside and there was heavy shielding within the dome, it was nevertheless audible; a high-pitched, almost unbearable piercing whistle that made the inner ears quiver and jump. In the corner, Kendra gasped and dug her fingers into her ears, moaning. Hubbs upped the amplitude. Kendra began to writhe and looked toward me, her mouth distorted. She said something, but of course I could not hear it. Nor can I lip-read. Then she turned and ran from the room, her gait wobbling and ungraceful. Of course. The noise would attack the middle ear.

I looked at the monitor. Hubbs was waving and screaming, probably in triumph, although hard to tell, gesturing wildly in that direction. On the monitor, the mounds, already crumpled, were now pulsating, as if something within them were in agony, and caused them to quiver as if they were living bodies, and the monitor, faithfully tracked into the motion, showed everything, the heaving, splitting apart, and final slow opening. Something porous and gelatinous came from the mounds and began to work its way across the desert. *My God,* Hubbs screamed, *the sons of bitches are alive, goddamnit,* and it certainly looked that way; it looked as if not only the mounds but the noise had acquired life and was now moving in agony across the desert floor. The piercing went higher and higher; it was an agony in the ears that traced its way through the coils of the body to the bowels, the groin; I felt as if the noise were tearing me apart, and if it was doing this to me, *what was it doing to the ants?* I thought this was the answer; this had been the answer all the time, and we too stupid to see it, but see it we now had: the creatures could be destroyed by the sheer force of noise; it broke open their communications network and—because they worked at the auditory level to communicate with one another—they were abnormally sensitive to sound. We had them: *we had them,* I thought and gave one triumphant scream that was inaudible over the greater sounds in the laboratory, looking at the monitor on which the shriveled and blackened bodies of ants were now passing in panorama. We had created a charnel house of the desert, and the monitor had gone crazy, tracking movement after movement, but it could not keep up with the corpses of the ants, heaped in little piles now: they were scurrying from a thousand outlets; from a million secret little passages, the ants were being driven by sound to light . . . and I screamed yet again, turning to Hubbs, and realized only then that he was bellowing and pointing frantically at the air-conditioning unit above us. His throat and mouth were working, but it was impossible to hear him; all that I could do was to follow his pointing finger, and then I realized that he must have been screaming for thirty seconds or more, but I was so caught up in my own ecstasy I heard nothing.

WARNING MALFUNCTION read jagged letters on a strip above the unit. I had never seen this before, never even been aware that the emergency unit in the computer would have such a signal, but there it was, there it was: WARNING MALFUNCTION, and even as I followed Hubbs's pointing, shaking finger, the letters glowed and then shifted. CIRCUITS OVERHEATING.

The circuits overheated. They had somehow contrived to knock down the air conditioner. Feebly, Hubbs was trying to do something with the unit, throw in one or another series of switches, but he could not work one-handed. His injured hand was being held in straight to his belly, and he was obviously in terrible pain, but I could hear nothing. The sound was still oscillating working its way up the last cycles toward inaudibility, and it was now a deep and profound pain that I felt, a pain that worked out from the network of the body into some generalized and indefinable sense of woe that racked me: I wanted to cry, but all the time I was fighting with myself, forcing myself; I went to the unit, pushed Hubbs out of the way, and tried to work with the switches myself. There was some kind of safety mechanism in here. I did not know where or what it was—my instructions had included little in relation to the equipment itself—but I was still fighting, fighting to find the switch that would throw in the emergency cooling unit and save us when—

—The unit exploded. The air conditioner literally blew up against my hand, little fibers and filters of smoke ripping out with a sound like tearing cloth, and I was able to hear this quite well, was able to hear everything because the screaming white noise stopped instantly. Of course it would, I thought; the sound generator was hooked into the air conditioner itself, for without the proper coolant the terrific heat generated by its functioning would cut off immediately. Be grateful, I thought, be grateful enough that it did stop, because the sound of the white noise unit under malfunction would probably have been quite enough to blow open an eardrum.

I looked over at Hubbs. He was weeping, holding his injured hand, frankly given over to sobs and little empty explosions of sound that were both more terrible and human than anything I had ever seen from the man. "I can't stand it," he was saying. "I just can't stand it anymore. They know everything; they

111

know everything about us." But I had no time to comfort him, no time to deal with him on any level. There was worse trouble. The abused air conditioner was suddenly on fire, throwing its deadly little fingers of flame into the air, and Kendra was suddenly by my side, a blanket in her hand. Together, we smothered the flames. Her motions were quick, efficient, instinctive: she worked with that sheer economy of motion and absence of panic that comes from the deepest part. It was stunning to see her work; I was amazed that after all she had been through she was able to deal with a situation in this fashion . . . and then, painfully it occurred to me as she helped me to wrap the blanket tightly against the heaving parts of the gutted unit . . . of course, of course she would be able to do this. There was no surprise in it at all. It was the first time, since the coming of the ants, that she had been able to use the knowledge she had.

And that was more frightening than anything.

Because the ants had one by one stripped all of us of our weapons.

VII

Everything in the station came in duplicate. Researchers, computers, monitors. Air conditioning and reserve. So after Lesko had gotten the fire extinguished in the gutted unit, he was able, under Hubbs's direction, to get the auxiliary started. Hubbs was too weak to perform the necessary splicing maneuvers himself. He stood there, sweat coming off his face in little, open rivers, looking at Lesko as he worked. The girl had gone to lean against a wall where she looked at them, her face soot-blackened, her eyes staring points of light, apparently too tired to talk. Hubbs no longer resented her. She was part of the environment with which they had to work, that was all. The ants were inimical to them and so was the girl; that was about the way that Hubbs's mind had calculated it, Lesko decided. Of course it was possible that he misunderstood the man, but he doubted it. He did not think there were any incalculables at all.

"I can't believe it," Hubbs said. He held his pained hand, looked out the window at the bodies of ants heaped like ash on the desert. "To know our plans, our strengths, our weaknesses . . . even the machine on which everything else depended. How could they know?"

"They knew," Lesko said.

"It's just not possible."

"It's completely possible," Lesko said. "Weren't you the one who predicated that they were intelligent, that they communicated with one another, that they controlled this situation? You were right." He finished a splice, turned a switch, and the auxiliary unit whined faintly, then began to catch. He felt cool air working its tentative way across the laboratory. "I wonder how long before they get to this one," he said.

"Stop it!" Hubbs said. His face was white. "Don't say that! We must not—"

"Be reasonable," Lesko said quietly. "You were the one who understood this from the first, weren't you? You said that they were an intelligent, functioning force, that we could develop communication with them, that they were probably aware of our purpose and our moves. You canceled out communications with base because you wanted to study them without interference. You wouldn't summon a helicopter because it might have gotten between you and your studies and the greater glory of the Coronado Institute." He looked at Hubbs closely; the man seemed to be dwindling under what Lesko was saying. All right. He deserved it. There was neither pity nor guilt; only implication. "You've sustained a bite, the extent of which we can't even determine because there's no way to get to medical aid. Also because of your desire to study without interference. There are three people dead out on the desert—"

"All right," Kendra said from the corner. "Leave him alone."

"Leave him alone?" Lesko said. Cool air was pouring through the laboratory; the thermometer had already dropped to below ninety. He felt the sweat beginning to dry on his forehead in streaks. "I wish I could leave him alone. Don't you know that he's responsible—"

"It doesn't matter," Kendra said. "Don't you see that? It doesn't matter who's responsible for anything; we've got to cooperate with one another. Otherwise we'll never—"

"That's a nice attitude," Lesko said. "That's really very touching. It's just your family—"

"Please, Jim," she said, quietly. Her eyes were intense; she seemed more self-possessed however than at any moment since he had seen her at the ranch. "You don't understand that it's all behind us now. Those things want to kill us. Unless we work together they're going to."

"She's right," Hubbs said in a small voice. "You

must listen to her. But she's wrong too. They don't want to kill us."

The computer cut in with a *whop!* Lesko heard the chattering. "They don't?" he said. "What do they want to do, then? Change our life-style?"

Hubbs, holding his wrist, looked at Lesko levelly, seriously. "I think that that's exactly what they want to do," he said. "If they had wanted to kill us, they could have done it at any time for the last day. Don't you realize that?"

"I don't realize anything," Lesko said. "I suggest that we take the jeep and try to get out of here. If we're very lucky, we just might make a run for it—"

"You really think so, James?" Hubbs said weakly. "Look."

They followed his finger pointing through the window. In the distance, they could see an object burning. A halo of black floated around the flames. Ants, of course. Burning ants.

"There's the jeep," Hubbs said.

"I told you," said Kendra quietly. "We must live or die here. There's nothing else to do."

"So what do you suggest we do," Lesko said to Hubbs. "You're the senior man; you're still in command. What do we *do* with them?"

"That's quite clear," Hubbs said. "We send them a message."

Kendra and Lesko stared at him. He held their gaze. "Do you see anything else?" he said.

Kendra began to laugh desperately.

"I still think that we can reach some kind of accommodation," Hubbs said.

Pain tore through him and as Lesko watched, he staggered.

VIII

Lesko's Diary: We worked desperately to get the computer back into operation and to work out a code that might be comprehensible to the ants. Three days ago, make it two, I would have thought this insanity: there we were, two Ph.D.s stranded in the desert, trying to strike up a conversation with a colony of ants who we believed to be intelligent. But Kendra's analysis of the situation had been completely correct; we were going to live or die in the station, and we could only deal on the terms we had left. Flight was hopeless, insecticide too laborious (the ants would only find an immune reaction), and communication with base had been destroyed. We could hope, and in fact did, that base would, after a while, become curious about the break in communication and would send out at least one helicopter, better yet a rescue team . . . but I knew base; I knew bureaucracy and levels of approval, and it was clear to me that by the time a request for emergency assistance had been bucked up the various levels of the chain of command and then bucked down again, several days might have elapsed. We were, after all, doing independent research, although government financed (this discrimination was important to the bureaucrats if not to me), and Hubbs's unremitting hostility to base would not count well for us. It could not possibly; their most understandable reaction would be to meet his hostility with apathy. If he wanted not to be bothered, then they would not bother him, and so on. So Kendra was right. She had been the first of us to see it. It was our world in that station; everything depended on us.

It depended upon us because I was increasingly convinced that the ants had far more in mind (and by this time I fell into Hubbs's pattern of thinking quite easily; this was a "mind" with which we were dealing) than simply overrunning the station. They could have done that at will days ago; for that matter, if this colony had chosen, it could have made our mission impossible simply by rendering the desert uninhabitable. They had *let* us come to Paradise City just as they had allowed the residents to flee. It was their terrain.

But what did they want us for? For what purpose had they allowed us to set up the station on the desert, prepare our computers, drop the insecticide? I had an idea that I kept to myself, seeing no point or purpose in bringing it to Hubbs's attention. He was a sick man and this would only have made him sicker; either that or it had occurred to him already, and he certainly would not need to hear it from me. That idea was quite simply that the ants needed our presence because they wanted *sample specimens* and that through their analysis of us, to say nothing of their analysis of the three corpses littering the desert floor, they would arrive at a clear, methodical plan of attack.

Not to think of it. Not to think of it. What I want to make clear is that all during the events that I am describing I did my best to swing clear of hysteria, to carve panic out of my mind, to function at a pure level of scientific detachment. If I had allowed the thoughts I am describing to enter into the forefront of consciousness, I am quite certain that none of us would have been able to have functioned at all . . .

but I did not, much of this occurred to me only after the fact, when I realized also that I had probably been dwelling on it subconsciously for a long time.

The instant task was all that had mattered. I shared Hubbs's obsession: we had to establish some kind of communication with the ants. If we could communicate with them, divine their purposes, find some one-to-one correspondence between language and activity, we might be able, if not to understand them, to at least find some point of weakness. We might even—this insane thought was rattling around, I admit, almost throughout—have the equivalent of a couple of Scotches together and discuss our mutual problems as any group of good fellows might. We had common interests, did we not? We were living tenants of the earth together; that miserable mudball in an exiled section of the Milky Way. Surely ant and man could coexist peacefully as against the greater common enemy without. We might even be able to voyage to the stars together, the ants developing a communications network that would implement our vast technological resources. Drink up, fellows; next round is on me. I am sure that I will be forgiven for this stream of consciousness; it could have happened to the best of you.

Hubbs became a little stronger as we worked on the communications problem. Kendra, meanwhile, left the laboratory to work in the galley. She seemed to have found her own means of dealing with the situation by placing herself into a domestic situation; she would do housekeeping while the men concentrated on the problems at hand. This did not concern me in the least; I was able to envy the profound instinct and sense of structure that she was able to bring to this. If women did the housekeeping and men the breadwinning in the ancient way, then surely the ants would relent. It was—I will admit this—pleasant to have her out of the way as we worked, because my feelings toward her had reached such a level of intensity by now that her mere presence was disturbing. Madness, perhaps, to entertain lustful thoughts while in the midst of what might have been a world crisis . . . but this is our nature, or at least my nature, God forgive me. Individual evolution, the primacy of the ego. It would have been better to have been a gestalt.

Hubbs at least could now be leaned upon. He was still in pain, but had somehow internalized it, and although his cheeks were bright with fever, his eyes were calm. He helped me feed a simple binary figure into the computer. Mathematics, the universal language. We would alternate *1* and *2* in rhythmic and irrhythmic powers, working on the channel of sound that seemed to be their belt; then we would clear channels for receptivity. Hubbs was pretty sure that if communication was established and the ants willing to meet us, they would hurl back our own signal at us *1* and *2* exactly as we had sent it. "I'm going to believe that the sons of bitches are reasonable and that they want to work with us," Hubbs said, working over the charts. "We may have a malevolent intelligence here, but I am going to assume for our immediate purposes that they have merely been trying to call our attention to them in order to establish communication, and when we do this, our purposes will have met theirs and the siege will stop. I will assume this because if it is *not* so, our problems are probably insuperable. Do you see what I mean, James?" I saw what he meant. I had made the same set of assumptions myself. We sent them our message in binary code.

And we waited.

IX

The queens accepted the signal. Glucose balances shifted; something happened in an almost electrical fashion, and a series of impulses were transferred from the queens to the soldiers. The soldiers had been burying their dead, thousands of them, in little depressions carved by the grenade near the towers. Now they stopped.

They picked up the signal from the queens.

And then, responsive, their cilia quivering, they advanced.

X

Lesko: NO CORRELATION

NO CORRELATION

NO CORRELATION

"What do they want?" he said. "What do they *want?*"

"They won't tell us," Hubbs said.

NO CORRELATION

"I know they're receiving," he said. "Activity is indicated. They're lying to us! They know we're communicating!"

NO CORRELATION

"Don't take this personally, James," Hubbs said. He was bent over the printout. Lesko could see the smooth slick spot at the back of his skull. "If they don't want to respond, it must be for other reasons."

NO CORRELATION

NO CORRELATION

"I'll kill them," Lesko said. He felt insanity working within his veins like blood, and it was a good feeling. Smash, injure, kill, he thought: it might be the only thing we know, but we know it well. "I think we should burn them," he said. "Go after them with the blue."

"It won't work, James," Hubbs said. He stood wearily, turned toward Lesko, his face as impenetrable as steel. Now he was the calmer one; the roles were shifting back and forth almost in a binary way themselves, Lesko thought. "We know that they are receiving, which is something. They can be reached. So if we can reach them now with something that can hurt—"

"No," Lesko said. "We tried that before."

"We'll have to try it again."

Kendra came into the room. "If you want something to eat, you can have it," she said. "You can—" and then she looked over at the monitor. The two men had ignored it, absorbed in the printout. Her eyes bulged.

She screamed.

Lesko turned, lunged toward her, and she fell into his grasp, her finger pointing at the monitor. "Look," she said. "Just look—" and he looked then as Hubbs also turned to look, Kendra falling back in his arms. He felt her full weight and thought for a moment that she had fainted, but then her feet scrambled for balance on the floor, and she righted herself. Strong. She was strong. There was a deer mouse on the monitor—

—A deer mouse lying on the desert, tongue hanging out of its mouth, twitching in final death agonies. From its ears, mouth, nose hung clusters of ants like little bouquets, and as Lesko watched, the mouse made one last frantic attempt to find purchase and then collapsed, writhed, died. The monitor tracked in to show the green and gold clusters of death. Kendra breathed against his neck. "It's horrible," she said. "They killed—" She could not go on.

NO CORRELATION

NO CORRELATION

"They don't want to listen to us," Hubbs said flatly. "They don't want any part of us at all. All that they want to do is to kill."

"I can't stand it," Kendra said quietly. "I can't—"

NO CORRELATION

NO CORRELATION

The deer mouse began to move.

It writhed again on the ground, but in a different fashion. The limbs did not seem coordinated; they worked against one another, off-balance, painfully. But even as they watched, the motions seemed to acquire smoothness and flow. To take on the appearance of efficiency. The green and gold of the body had now become a deep red as burst blood vessels carried their contents near the surface.

The mouse rolled and began to walk.

It walked across the desert, parading for the monitor in a way that no mouse had ever walked before, all limbs stiff, head forward, dead eyes glazed with the light of the sun. It headed toward one of the broken towers. It moved quite rapidly. The new mode of locomotion might be unmouselike, but you had to give the ants credit: they knew the locomotor facilities.

The mouse went rapidly, proudly, into the nearest of the towers and disappeared from the monitor. The monitor, disengaged, tracked back, and showed another deer mouse writhing on the sand.

"Mother of God," Hubbs said. "Mother of God." He sounded quite reverent.

Holding Kendra, Lesko walked her quietly from the laboratory and into the bedroom where he lay her on the cot.

When he returned to the laboratory, Hubbs had collapsed or, more likely, fallen asleep against one of the shelves, a strange, broken grin on his face.

Lesko turned off the monitor and went out of there.

PHASE IV

Lesko's Diary: When I awakened from a tortured nap, it could not have been more than an hour later, Hubbs himself was awake, suffering, and delirious. While I had been sleeping, Kendra had moved him from the laboratory to the cot we had given her and was attending him with a cold towel and a glass of water, while he thrashed and moaned on the sheets. I felt his forehead. It seemed to be a fever of a hundred and three, a hundred and four. There was just nothing to do.

"Take some water," Kendra said to Hubbs and looked at me pleading, desperate. Hubbs pushed the water away. She put the cloth into the glass and gently wiped his forehead, and his eyes cleared a little. "Sick," she said. "He's awfully—"

"I know," I said.

"We've got to get him out of here."

"We've all got to get out of here," I said. "I just don't know how." I was in a peculiar numb state where one can respond intelligently enough to all queries without being able to initiate anything. Now I looked at Kendra, unspeaking. "He is awfully sick," I said, going back to that.

"Analysis," Hubbs said in a thin voice, moving his head back and forth.

"What?" Kendra said, leaning over, mopping his brow again.

"It's clear they have failed," Hubbs said and stopped, took in a gasping breath, went on then. "They have failed to achieve—"

"Is there something you want?" she said. I touched her wrist gently, and she brought it back.

"Let him talk," I said. I leaned over. "What have they failed to achieve?" I said. "They have taken—"

"No," he said, and the shaking and twitching of his head began again. "They will have to learn that we have made up our minds—"

"Would you like something?" Kendra said. "If you want—"

"Please," I said. I had gotten it into my head that Hubbs had something approaching an answer. Was it his delirium or mine? Who was to know. "He's trying to say something!"

Hurt, she went back, still holding the towel.

"We will have to tell them," Hubbs said with terrible clarity, "that we are willing to pay the price. They understand who we are, what we are doing; and we will make them know that humanity itself will not suffer—"

"I'm going to play the radio," Kendra said. She must have been slightly delirious herself. Understandable, understandable; everything comes together. "Music will make him feel better," she said. "If only we can have a little music—"

She put on a console that was resting on an overhead shelf. I turned to tell her that communications were broken, that we could hear nothing, but was overwhelmed by the noise pouring out from the radio. It was the sounds of the ants. I could hear cilia cracking, the fine, slow, high beep of their communication.

"What is that?" I said and reached toward her.

"It's only music," she said. "It's—"

I decided that she had gone insane. I reached out and hit her across the face, gently, but with enough sting in the follow through to leave a slight imprint. She gasped, backed away from me.

"Don't you hear that?" I said. "Kendra, don't you—"

Understanding came into her face. Something crumpled in her expression, and she heard the radio. "Oh, my God," she said. "It isn't music. It's—"

"Of course it is," Hubbs said. He had come off the couch and was standing there, weaving drunkenly. "How do you think that they were able to pick up on us?"

"Oh, my God," Kendra said. She dropped the towel and turned toward the door.

"Not so fast," Hubbs said. He was clearly delirious. He raised a hand and Kendra stopped. "Who did this?" he said. "Who set up the radio?"

"Hubbs—" I said.

The ant noises were louder yet. They moved up and down the scale of pitch, *F-sharp major,* I thought with lunatic precision. They sounded quite cheerful, considering the point of origin.

"You lousy bitch," Hubbs said. "You set us up for

this. You did it, didn't you? Until you came to the station everything was fine. We had them on the run. You're their agent."

Kendra's hand was against her cheek. "No," she said. "No, that's not so." I knew that this was not so. I reached an arm out toward her.

"Don't listen," I said. "He's crazy. He's sick. He's—"

"You're crazy," she said. "You're both crazy! *You're both crazy!*" She turned and ran from the room, stumbling against a wall. Hubbs reached toward her, but I restrained him. I could hear her shrieks all the way down the hall, and then a door slammed.

"Let me at her," Hubbs said wildly. "Let me at her now. I am not helpless. I will not be humiliated. I will not allow humanity to be vanquished by a group of ants. I am humanity's representative, and they cannot do this to me." He broke from my grip with maniacal strength and stumbled toward the shelf on which the radio was perched, still singing crisply away. He reached out a hand, seized the trembling wire.

He pulled it and the radio fell.

It fell to his feet, exploding with a fierce crash, little sparks and dazzling intimations of flame pouring from it, and Hubbs screamed with the heat and the impact, the scream turning into an *ah!* of satisfaction as he kicked the radio toward the wall. "Now!" he said. "Now let's see if they can trace us!" and he lost his balance, a flame of illness going through him, collapsed against the shelf . . . and upset about twenty thousand dollars' worth of technical equipment. Wires, tubing, coils, computer leads, burners, jars, dials, indices, thermometers fell from the shelf and exploded on the floor in a shower of translucence. Hubbs looked down at this with a slightly bemused expres-

127

sion, seemed almost clownish. "Oh, for heaven's sake," he said. "I didn't mean to do that." Then something caught his attention on the floor. "Ah," he said. "Aha!" He dropped to his knees, heedless of the glass splinters . . . and began to crawl.

I knew he was mad. Of course he was mad. But his insanity at that moment was no greater than my own. I could only think: *wouldn't it be strange if Kendra were indeed the agent?* Then the madness went away like a blanket ripped off as I saw what Hubbs was doing.

There was, somewhere in the coils and splinters on the floor, an ant speeding through, probably from the radio, which was still sputtering. Hubbs reached forward, his face alight, and then with a terrific scream brought his fist down on the ant. "I've got him!" he said. *"I've got him now!"* His face distorted, and I reached to pull him from the wreckage, hopelessly bellowing Kendra's name, needing someone to take the burden of madness with me, and suddenly she was there. She had not fled into the desert after all. Together the two of us, struggling, were able to lift Hubbs to his feet and carry him out of the laboratory, down the corridor. "Look," Hubbs whispered to me. He raised his hand slowly, then opened it fully. In the palm, I could see the pearl of a blood spot.

"I got him," he said. Then he looked at Kendra. "I got him," he said again. "Don't you see? I *got* him. You aren't the enemy. He is. Deeply apologize. Regret my terrible error. Most unscientific of me, really. . . ." And then he fainted quite neatly in her arms. I laid him on the floor while Kendra went back to the laboratory to get the cloth and the water, still fixated, no doubt, on the thought that if Hubbs could be brought back to his senses we might all, somehow, obtain release. She returned as I was leaning over him, Hubbs now prostrated on the floor, his eyes closing again. "I'm sorry," she said and put the water down. "I'm sorry."

She reached toward me and for one blank instant I thought she was going to touch, had no idea what madness had possessed her (were we going to copulate on this floor before Hubbs, howling screams of defiance to the ants?), and then she had turned, she was running, she was moving down the hall again and once more that sound of the slamming door.

"I'm terribly sorry," Hubbs said in delirium on the floor. "All wrong, all wrong. Sorry—"

"Enough," I said. "Enough, enough." Enough of Hubbs, enough of ants, enough of delirium; I got up swaying and went down the hall, found the door where Kendra had bolted inward, and opened it to find her in the emergency access, sobbing against a wall, her body tilted in a crooked position. Like the field mouse. I reached toward her and touched her shoulder blade. She quivered once like a bird and then was still.

She came against me, her face into my chest. "I'm sorry," she said. "I'm just so sorry." And I said it's all right, it's all right, meaningless, stupid babble I am sure, the things we can say to one another only when the situation has gone beyond words, and finally she was quiescent against me, and I could feel the slow pulse in the back of her neck as I rubbed it gently.

"Just hold me now," she said. "Just hold me."

I held her.

Otherwise, there was nothing at all.

II

"I want to apologize if I was irrational during the day," Hubbs said. He was sitting on the pallet, and although he looked devastated, the fever had gone. He reached out, touched Kendra's hand once, then turned toward Lesko. "I'm sorry. Everything has gone wrong." He took a small sip of water, finishing the glass; Kendra took it from his hand and went into the galley for a refill. Lesko could hear the sound of the tap running; at least that was still working. Although God knew what if anything the ants had done to the chemistry. . . .

"Why don't they kill us?" Lesko said. All the emotions of the day had gone from him; now like Hubbs he felt that he was looking down a long, flat tunnel of possibility, gray on either side. Cool breezes in the shaftway. "They roast us by day, dare us to come out at night . . . why play games with us? What do they want? What do they want?"

Hubbs ran Kendra's towel across his face. He seemed to have lost twenty pounds since his delirium, but his face was lucid and clear. "I've been thinking about caste," he said. "Specialization among special insects."

"Enough," Lesko said. He stood, looked through the window. Now and then a spurt of flame came off the desert, showing a suggestion of moving forms.

Otherwise, a stillness. He had a feeling of having arrived at some end. "Take it easy and try to go to sleep. Maybe the helicopter will be here in the morning."

"Never," Hubbs said. "They hate us back there. As far as they're concerned, we're merely boondoggling a special grant for some kind of esoteric research, and God forgive me, James, I encouraged that feeling. I wanted it that way; I felt that the more contempt they felt, the less interference we would find . . . and you see how successful that plan has been. No, we've got to deal with this here. On our own. We will win or we will lose . . . but fate is being decided here."

"Don't be that dramatic," Lesko said. "It's only our deaths that are at issue here."

"Do you believe that, James?" Hubbs said. He looked up at Lesko. "Do you really believe that at all?"

Lesko shook his head and looked away from the window. "No," he said. "I do not. But it felt better."

"I understand. But look," Hubbs said quietly. "In every ant colony, there are clear segments, divisions, a hierarchy if you will. There are workers, winged males who are also soldiers . . . and there is the queen."

"Presumably."

"Ants are organized around the queen," Hubbs said quietly. "She is immobile, powerless, except for the terrific force that she exerts upon these workers. She controls them and that is her power. They keep her alive, maintain her, and she is their heart and soul."

"All right."

"The heart and soul of their lives," Hubbs said. "And whatever we are dealing with, these are still ants just as you and I would always be men. Some-where," he said flatly, "there must be a queen."

Lesko stood quietly, saying nothing. Just barely conscious of the fact that he had been waiting for the sound; a door creaked and Kendra came in, holding a fresh glass of water. She sat by Hubbs and helped him drink in small, greedy gulps, looking at him with compassion. Lesko reached out and took her hand. She left it in his palm, unresisting.

"If she died," Hubbs said, "discipline and organiza-tion would crumple. Chaos would result. They would no longer be able to function, and we would prevail after all."

Kendra fed him more water. Lesko felt her hand, the firm surfaces leaving an impression upon his palm. He decided that on balance he liked Hubbs after all; the man was reacting with rare courage, he had more spiritual reserves than anyone would have calculated . . . but it was academic. All of this was. "The war's over," he said.

"Is it?"

"It has to be. They have the power," Lesko said. "The only hope left is if our message somehow re-gistered on them." He paused. "And if they decide in their infinite mercy that we're worth keeping alive."

"You're projecting a human emotion upon the ir-relevant and the inhumane," Hubbs said calmly. He pushed Kendra's hand away without repudiation, simply as if he were doing it for emphasis. "I think that I could locate this queen and kill her."

"That's ridiculous," Kendra said suddenly. "You're very sick."

"I'm not so sick that I can't move. If we can find her, get a location from the transmitter, then I can track her. I'm not asking you to do this." He coughed spasmodically; Kendra gave him more water. "I'm going to die, anyway," Hubbs said. "I'm sure that the infection I've received is fatal; it's just a matter of going in and out of delirium now, of various spells of weakness. The next time I may not recover. I'm willing to take this on myself. I'm not asking anyone else to do it."

"We can't locate the queen," Lesko said.

"I think we can," said Hubbs. He stood, weaving, then walked toward the door. "I'm going to go to the laboratory," he said. "Is anyone going to come with me?"

"No," Kendra said. "It's not worth it. You can live. You can go on. You don't have to do this—"

"Live?" Hubbs said at the door. "Go on? How long do you think we have, unless we do something desperate?" He stood still, Lesko and Kendra looking at him silently. "It's not only us," he said quietly. "Don't you see that now? The stakes have gone far, far beyond Paradise City and what is going on within this enclosure. They want the world. The only way is to kill their queen." He walked away, leaving Lesko and Kendra standing there.

"He's quite right, you know," Lesko said. "We're doomed."

"We may be doomed," she said. "In fact, I know we're doomed, but he can't go out there; he can't attack them, he—"

"Yes, he can," Lesko said quietly. "And he's going to. I've got to help him."

"I think you're crazy," Kendra said. She said it quietly, there was less accusation than simply knowledge in her voice. "I think that all of you scientists are crazy."

"That may well be true," said Lesko. "But it would

133

have to be this way. Products of individual evolution. *Everybody's* crazy, you know."

He walked from the room.

After a time she followed him.

III

Up the corridor swung the invasion force guided by signals from its queen, through the darker pits and lighter pits of the enclosure, through the dusky caves where small objects hung from the ceiling like rope, through the slick, smooth walls themselves, and into the river, up the river for a while, and then into that large, damp enclosure where it nestled in comfortably, looking through the tunnels of light before it. Within its antennae, it felt the sounds of contentment from the queen, and waves of longing and pleasure came back from it in response as it hooked its cilia into the overhang and waited there, poised, ready to die for its queen, ready to live for its queen. . . .

Something joggled it momentarily, but it hung on and then the joggling stopped.

"What's going on, Kendra?" a voice said.

"I had an itch," another voice said. "It felt like something was inside me. But now it's stopped."

The queen purred.

IV

"They're sending us a message," Hubbs said.

Lesko walked over there. How many times had he walked through this laboratory to Hubbs's side to see some horror? But this in its way was the worst of all. The printout was coming from the computer smoothly, evenly: over the printout a stylus was working, drawing a symbol on the empty paper, filling it with one repeated figure drawn over and over again. The stylus seemed to be gripped by some invisible but ritualistic hand, the figuring was neat, the movements precise and contained. It went on. A circle, then a shift of the stylus, and a dot. Circle and a dot. Circle and a dot. Lesko looked at it.

"They've found our channel," Hubbs said. "Fair enough. We found theirs, so they found ours. She's speaking to us."

"Who?"

"Who?" Hubbs said and held his enlarged arm, which now could not move without support. "The queen," he said.

Lesko looked at the printout. Circle and dot. Circle and dot. Circle and—"What does it mean?" he said.

"Think."

"A circle with a dot. What does it mean?"

"It doesn't matter," Hubbs said. "I don't care anymore." He fumbled with the monitor, worked the tracking mechanism. "I'm going to try and locate the queen while she's diverted. I think I know where to look now." He put the monitor on manual, tracked the camera laboriously.

Circle. Circle and dot. Lesko looked at it, feeling the sweat again and his heartbeat. Heartbeat. *Dah-dit. Dah-dit.* Circle and dot. Dah dit. Circle and—

"We'll find her," Hubbs said quietly. "It's attuned to size now, not movement. I know what we're looking for now—"

"Circle and dot," Lesko said. He was trying to think of something else, but his mind was blunted; he could see only what was feeding out ahead of him in the printout. Hypnosis, perhaps. The ants had control over their minds as well. But there was something terribly important, something he could not quite locate. . . . "Circle enclosing a dot," he said. "Now I know how a rat feels in a maze. We're rats in a maze. Wait a minute," he said after a pause, feeling a vague, pulsing excitement. "Just wait a moment." The shackles seemed to be breaking; he could think again. "I think I see something."

"Um," Hubbs said, twirling the monitor, completely absorbed. "Of course. Where has that girl gone?" He squinted into the screen.

"Listen," Lesko said. "We're subjected to various stimuli and then we're allowed our response. It's almost like a controlled experiment in which *we* are the subjects."

"That's interesting," Hubbs said. "Of course it has nothing to do with finding the queen. . . ."

"Almost as if," Lesko went on, "they wanted to find out which rat was the strongest . . . or the smartest."

"Smartest?"

"It's an intelligence test," Lesko said. "We're being subjected to an intelligence test."

"Ah," Hubbs said, abstractedly. The breaking of the fever and his absorption with the monitor seemed to have restored his scientific mode. "That's interesting, James, although it means nothing."

"Nothing? Don't you see what's happening? We're not checking them? They're evaluating *us!*"

"Then they're in for a surprise," Hubbs said. "Because I'm going to find their queen and disevaluate them."

Kendra came into the laboratory. She looked disheveled. Lesko looked at her and extended his arm. She huddled against him and he held her in. "Look at this," he said pointing to the tracing. "They're sending us a message after all. Do you know what it represents?"

"I was frightened," she said.

"We're all frightened," said Hubbs at the monitor. "But we're going to go on, anyway."

"What could the circle and the dot represent?" Lesko said again.

"Could it be this place?" Kendra said. Her eyes widened as if she only had realized then what she was saying. "*This place?*"

"I think you're right," Lesko said after a pause. She trembled; he held her more tightly. "Of course . . . but what then would the dot represent?"

"Something they want?" she said.

He inhaled slowly and then breathed out air. "Someone they want," he said. "This place and someone they want."

"I think I've found their queen," Hubbs said. "I think that I'm closing in on her now."

"Something the ants want?" Kendra said as if hypnotized. "They want someone from this place? Is that it?"

"Yes," Lesko said quietly. "I think that that's it. But what could they want? Who?"

"You think they want someone," she said. He could feel the tremor in her body. "You really do?"

"That was what you said."

"But why would they want someone?"

He stared at her and said, "They would want someone to talk to them."

"It doesn't matter," Hubbs said again. "None of that matters. A frontal attack is the only answer. We are long past the stage of negotiation."

Kendra ignored this. "You mean they might be angry at someone who did them some harm?"

"I don't know," Lesko said. *Circle and dot. Circle and dot.* Fluidly, the tracings poured out.

"I didn't mean to hurt them," she said. "It was an accident. I was upset. I didn't mean to smash the container, but it just happened." Her eyes were black. "They couldn't want to hurt me," she said. Her body fluttered. "They've got to understand—"

"Please, Kendra," Lesko said. "They don't want you. They want only communication of some kind. They don't want to hurt anyone."

"I didn't mean it," she said. "I didn't mean to hurt them. It was an accident, that was all it was." *Circle and dot.* "No," she said then. "You can't protect me. No one can. They're going to get what they want."

"You're wrong, Kendra."

"What would they do with that person if he came out and tried to talk with them?" Kendra said. *Circle and dot.*

"I don't know," Lesko said.

"If that person explained what had happened and

offered to try and help them . . . would the ants be kind?"

"I don't know that either."

"Would they let the others go free?"

Lesko slowly turned his head, looked at her. Her face was luminous and sad. "Kendra—" he said.

"If they would let the others go free, then I would go to them," she said.

"Please—" he said to her and then did not know what he would have said then because Hubbs was suddenly bellowing with triumph over in his corner. Lesko gently moved from Kendra and looked at the man. He was standing, holding his glasses, his face triumphant.

"Come here, James," he said. "I've got their queen."

He walked over to Hubbs.

And behind him, Kendra left the laboratory.

He did not even see her go.

V

On the monitor, tracking in extreme closeup, Lesko could see a low range of what appeared to be mountains; amidst those mountains were three dead volcanoes. The mounds, of course, enormously magnified. The volcanoes were spaced evenly apart and before them was what seemed to be a faint oblong shape, rising in outline through the sound.

Hubbs touched him on the shoulder and Lesko jumped.

"She's in there," Hubbs said.

Lesko stared at him and then looked back at the monitor. Was it in his mind or did he detect a faint movement?"

"I'm going to get her," Hubbs said.

VĪ

Kendra thought, Oh, it was a lovely evening, just a lovely evening for a little walk on the desert, and she wished that she had thought of this before, long before, just a quiet walk on the desert, a stroll through the sands to get her thoughts in order. Lesko, the younger one, was attractive and maybe she had been distracted by him, but lustful thoughts were the antithesis of beauty, and it was beauty that she was seeking, beauty on the desert, and so she walked from the hatch into the clear, cold air, feeling the breeze ruffle her, and she wished that she had done this a long time ago, walk away from it, that was, be on her own so she would have a chance to get her thoughts in order without this distraction. Everybody was trying to distract her, but now freed of lustful thoughts, she could take a little stroll on the desert and decide what to do next. Maybe she could talk things over with the ants, even. Certainly, there was nothing that they could not work out together if only she could show them that she was a good person, as good as they were. Not that they were persons of course. All right, she would remember that. But they were lovely things.

What a nice evening, what a lovely evening, she murmured, feeling the wind blow through her hair as she walked along. She seemed to be stumbling a little, something wrong with her balance. Not enough fresh air, that was all. Too much being cooped up in that stultifying laboratory, thinking lustful thoughts, when all the time she could have been out in the cold, clear air. She felt song burble within her and let it come out, trailing her sounds to the heavens. How lovely, how profoundly mystic the heavens were! why she had never thought there were so many stars. How sweet to walk in the pilgrim's way, she sang, leaning on the everlasting arms, a snatch of hymn that she had heard, must have heard when she was a child, just a little girl with her horse Ginger, Ginger and she in the pilgrim's way together. How bright the path grows from day to day, leaning on the everlasting path, the hymn went on, and she sang it with a lovely lilt, admiring her voice; how sweet it was to be singing hymns in the desert, free of lust, free at last. She stopped. Something nestled against her toe and brought her to a halt before she fell. She stood there weaving, confused (were they out to get her, even in the desert? but what then of poor Clete and her grandparents; would they allow her to be assaulted here?), and looked down toward her feet, her adorable little feet someone had once called them, the toes like firm little cylinders balancing her on the sand . . . and from between them an ant had appeared. She looked down upon it. Hello, little friend.

Amazing how benign she felt toward the ants. It

had hardly been their fault that these terrible things had happened to her. No, it was all those lustful thoughts obsessing her, to say nothing of the bad air in the laboratory. Poor housekeeping. "Hello, little friend," she said, looking down at the ant. *How sweet to walk in the pilgrim's way.* Circle and dot. "I want you to listen." Her voice felt faint, speaking was an effort. Thin desert air, of course. Whoever got the idea that desert air was *good* for the lungs? Hers were parched. "Please listen to me," she said.

The ant stood between her toes in what she took to be a polite posture of attention. It was listening to her. All of the ants were her little friends now, and she was going to explain to them exactly what was on her mind and what she could do for them, and thus would be inaugurated a new era of peaceful cooperation. Between her and the ants, and as for those two lustful types in the laboratory, she could send them right to hell. *Hell.* Funny the words in which she was thinking. Ordinarily, she cursed. Very unusual circumstances of course. "I'm not afraid of you," she said to the ant. "We can work together."

The ant bit her.

The pain was so terrible it sent tears to her eyes, and she realized that she was standing on a desert, weakened as if by a terrible siege, babbling to herself, suffering from extreme pain. She raised her foot. The pain was terrific. It went through her in delicate pulsations, increasing. Was this what Hubbs had felt? Oh, how terrible if he had felt this way! "Why," she said to the ant. "Why did you do this to me?" and the ant bit her again.

She screamed and tried to hobble away. *In the pilgrim's way.* She had to get back to the laboratory and tell them what had happened. Only they could help her; *she had to get back*. Pain went through the foot on the ground. The ant had bitten her there.

She fell to the ground. The pain was absolutely paralyzing. She could not move. "Why are you doing this to me?" she said. "My God, why are you doing it?" She extended a hand. The ant bit her on the palm. Blood rose and she felt nausea. "I didn't want to hurt you!" she cried. "I thought that we could be friends; I thought that we could work together!" And then the biting came over her again: the ant or maybe it was ants by this time, a mass of them attacking (she could not tell; she could tell nothing) were swarming, raging, moving over her; she felt the bites like welts rising all over her body, and with each of them that terrible clarity increased. She could see everything now. She understood everything. Kendra rolled on her back, looked up at the sky, immobile as a tree trunk, and the ants went to work all over her body.

"I see," she said, her voice distinct, feeling herself beginning to depart from the pain as if a different, intact Kendra was rising and rising, flat to the sky, as large as a spaceship, covering the stars. "I see now. We could never have worked together, could we? Because what you want and what we want is entirely different and always would be. We would have to be enemies, wouldn't we? We would have to destroy one another."

The bites were gentle now, almost as if soporifics were being injected into her system, and she was no longer on the desert. She was floating free. She was no longer Kendra but something both more and less than Kendra, floating, detached, ascending. In that ascension she saw everything: for a stricken moment

143

she knew everything that had happened to her and what was happening next, and then peace covered her like a shroud and for a while, in that way, she felt nothing at all, awaiting the next and final phase.

VII

The colony fed.

VIII

Lesko's Diary: I did not even notice that Kendra had gone until minutes had elapsed and by that time it was too late to follow her: where would I have looked? Where, after all, would she be, and what could I have done? I realize that these questions have the aspect of rationalization, but my position must be made clear; this journal will be found some-day, I have great faith in that if nothing else, and it is important that my position be made absolutely clear because if nothing else I will stand by my genuine and sincere feelings for this girl (who has touched me profoundly) and my belief that there was nothing, absolutely nothing that I could have done once I realized that she had left the laboratory, was no longer in the station. Hubbs was struggling with his boots, groaning, grunting. "Where are the grenades?" he said. He was serious. The man was serious. He was out to destroy the queen.

"You used them up when you destroyed the towers," I said to him, looking at the monitor, looking through the windows to see if there was any trace of Kendra. She might well have wandered out upon the desert, and if I had seen any evidence of this, any trace of her whereabouts either through window or monitor, I would have pursued her whatever the risks, but I did not and what was the point? I had to help Hubbs. I had to stand by Hubbs. His condition was disastrous, his mission desperate, what would it have benefited any of us—assuming that Kendra was dead— for two to have gone wandering out on the desert to be assaulted and killed by the ants while the third carried on alone? I believed this. I believe it even now. This is not reason but common, scientific fact; a logical intelligence at work, the product of individual evolution. I believe that I am going mad.

"They couldn't," Hubbs said, grunting, trying to get on his equipment. "All of them?"

"Every one," I said. I continued to work the monitors and at the same time to make my notes in this journal. I wanted to get it up to date as rapidly as possible, because I had the feeling that I might not be writing much longer. Things seemed to be struggling on the desert floor again. "There isn't a grenade in the house," I said and giggled.

"Well," Hubbs said. "We'll have to devise something else." Suddenly he stopped struggling, looked at me with a despairing expression. "James?" he said. "I can't seem to get on my boots."

I looked at him and some comprehension of the absurdity of our position must have worked its way into me before it departed again. I went back to the monitor. "Please, James," he said. "You're going to have to give me some help with these; I can't go bootless onto the desert. They'll attack me."

"You know?" I said, looking at him, "you're talking about going out of here, getting through that circle, tramping miles through the desert, destroying an ant colony full of malevolent, poisonous ants that are presided over by a monstrous queen . . . but you can't even get your boots on."

"James——"

"Sit down, Hubbs," I said. "It won't work. The only thing to do is to continue working on the area of communications and try to hit them either on the noise belt or with a message of some sort. That's the only way——"

Hubbs snatched the paper out of my hands, crushed it, and threw it, trembling, against a wall. "No," he said.

I could have killed him then, but it was only—I realized this instantly—what the ants wanted. It would have saved them the trouble. I sat there, gripping the sides of the chair and said again, "It's hopeless, Hubbs."

"No, it isn't. I am going to show them. I will show them that man will not give in." He was crying.

"Did I tell you?" I said, through his sobs. "I was able to figure out their first message. With Kendra's help. Didn't you hear? The circle is this place and the dot is you. They want you."

"Or one of us."

"Oh, no," I said, shaking my head. I felt a manic certainty. "Kendra made that mistake and that's why she's lost out there somewhere. She thought that anyone would do. But it's only you, Hubbs. It was you all the time. You're our leader. How they respect you!"

"Then they're going to have me," Hubbs said.

He staggered back to his chair and tried once again to put his boots on. Hopeless. The man, drained by delirium, shaken by obsession, could no longer function. He collapsed over himself, mumbling like an old man. And something hit the windows.

It hit with a hard, spattering sound, opening into an aqueous rush. I looked out and saw that liquefied matter of some sort was striking us. The source seemed to be the mounds, but it was hard to tell. The monitor itself, the camera covered with the substance, had gone blank. A shrill keening began again. The patches hitting the windows were becoming darker. They looked like nothing more than liquefied human flesh.

Hubbs stood. He was not weaving. "That's it," he said. "There has to be an end to this. It will not go on any longer." His voice was very steady. "Do you see it now, James?" he said. "You must help me."

He pointed to his boots. The barrage had stopped; the desert hung clear before us like a painting. "Help me," he said.

I helped him.

IX

Through the monitor Lesko was able to follow
Hubbs's walk toward the mounds. He had wanted to
go with him, but Hubbs had said no, this was ridiculous. "The girl is dead," he said. "Don't you know
that, James? And if they kill the two of us then there
will be no one left to defend humanity. It's only
you and I against them now, James, and we must
have at least two chances; we can't let them have both
of us at once. If nothing else, we're buying time. I
will go and if I don't succeed, you can try it your
way. Goodbye, James. This is the way it must be,"
and then Hubbs had gone quickly through the hatch.
Lesko had let him go. The point was that the man
was absolutely right. Kendra was dead and all of the
others were dead and the ants had won everything
. . . but they still had the two wild cards, their individual chances to destroy the mounds of the queen, and
he could not halve their chances. He let the old
man go. He watched through the monitor.

Hubbs walked through the desert, confident for a
while, his stride steadier than it had been in days. In
his hand, he carried the dead grenade launcher, large
enough, heavy enough, blunt enough to strike the
queen's mound a killing blow . . . if he could get
there. He waved once or twice, looking almost jaunty,
the monitor picking him up in the colors of blood that

still streaked the lenses of the camera, and Lesko, his hands curled, studying the monitor intently, allowed himself the wild thought that Hubbs was going to *get through* . . . that the man was going to make it; he would destroy the queen's mound and with it the network of the colony. It was a tribute to humanity, that was all it was, this wracked, broken, trembling man, suffering from fever and a fatal infection, was still alive, still out there on the desert . . . moving implacably toward his goal. It's man! Lesko found himself thinking; it's the unconquerable human spirit, and what indeed was there to say about a man like Hubbs who had placed loyalty to his fellow creatures above loyalty to himself, heading out there bravely, the last defender as it were of millions of years of evolution, and Lesko thought he was going to make it, going to make it, Hubbs waved at him again through the monitor and then stopped, pointing downward. He had reached the mound. He raised the grenade launcher over his head.

Lesko held his breath.

And a swarm of ants came out of the mound.

They were red and green, these ants, the monitor, rushing in to track them, showing that telltale spot of yellow on their bellies, that luminiscent pearl of immunity, and as they came out of the mound in a swarm, Lesko realized that he had underestimated their numbers all of the time; not only had they misjudged the situation entirely . . . they had misjudged the number of queens. There was not one queen; there were probably a hundred nestled under the surfaces of the desert . . . and then he gave a great despairing cry because the ants were all over Hubbs now, hundreds, thousands, millions, swarming and thrusting their bodies at him until he was a solid jellied mass of green and red, and then the thing on the sands trembled and fell, the launcher also, ant-covered, falling away from him, and as Lesko watched in a kind of suspended attention, feeling linked to the monitor as if he were merely another ingredient within it, the mass on the ground ceased to struggle and then diminished. The bulge of red and green became a carpet of red and green.

The ants were feeding.

And as he watched, they consumed Hubbs.

In the last of the blood streaks, he saw the ants lying satiated on the desert as far as the monitor's range could cover, a solid, beautiful layer of green and red under the twinkling stars, and he cried then: did not cry for Hubbs so much—because Hubbs was already dead, had been dead from the moment he had left the hatchway, if not long before that—but for millions of years of evolution that everyone had believed in, poor stricken creatures, as being the will of Creation and Eternity . . . and which were now, it was quite obvious to Lesko, merely a twitch, an aberration, a little mistake that was being rectified cosmically before it could have gotten out of hand.

"Damn you!" he said. "Goddamn you all!" But he knew what he was talking of, and it was not the ants, and because it was the only responsible posture after all, he found himself laughing as the monitor showed the towers seal up and begin to grow at an enormous rate as if waving in triumph. . . .

X

Lesko's Diary: But even now as I sit here, writing the last of this, bringing it up to date and beyond, working out the final moves, I would still like to believe, and this is the paramount insanity, that given time, we could have come to some kind of understanding. They cannot regard us so cheaply. We may have been a mistake, but we were an *elegant* mistake, goddamn it. We had our points. We had things to say in our behalf. Even if it was only a misjudgment, something gone wrong in the flux of things, and it should have been the ants all the time . . . there were the pyramids, Shakespeare, Beethoven, Einstein, quasar theory, the Coronado Institute, the very species of intelligence that has, at the least, enabled me to identify exactly what has happened to us. . . .

Doesn't this count? Doesn't it count in our behalf? Maybe we were the wrong inheritors of the planet and after a few million years the Creator has come around to restore the balance; even so we had our points. I find it necessary to believe this. Could the ants compose a fugue or write *War and Peace?* How would they make out in ballet? How would they choreograph or play the flute? Of course I am delirious, but these are legitimate questions. *We cannot be shoveled off so cheaply*.

But of course we can. Of course we can. That is

exactly the point. There is no rational accommodation of interests; there is no agreement. We are an aberration to them, and there is no more possibility of dialogue than an exterminator would consider a dialogue with roaches before unleashing his spray can and paint. *We do not even exist to them.* And there is going to be no agreement of any sort. *They may not even see us.*

Sitting here over the last few hours—they have not overrun the station, they have all the time in the world, perhaps they are merely awaiting final instructions or then again they may relish this—I have made some calculations about their rate of expansion, using their intelligence, their powers of organization, their network of communications, and my general knowledge. Knowledge of their poisons, their ability to adapt genetically, and the control factors that underlie their activities; I believe that after this test run they will move rather quickly into other desert areas, taking over the countryside first and then laying siege to the towns and the cities. I believe that they will learn as they advance, anticipating our moves and always staying a move ahead, and as best as I can calculate, we have—all of us, Siberians, Eskimos, housewives in Dayton, Ohio, *all of us*—perhaps two more months.

Or perhaps far less if this is merely a dry run for certain techniques that they will put into immediate production.

We have only one chance, which is no chance at all, and yet it would be to utterly give up not to take it . . . and that is the counterattack suggested by Hubbs and which he gave his life for . . . a direct assault on their queen. I know that they are going to do to me what has been done to him and that there cannot be more than ten minutes of life as I know it remaining to me . . . but I am writing these last lines with my boots on, my heavy gear, holding another grenade launcher and a rifle at the ready . . . and I am going to go out there and try it as well.

I wish that it weren't me. I wish that none of this had ever happened. I wish that it were all a dream, just as our very presence on this planet has, to those cosmic forces, been a dream and that I could rectify it, just as they have rectified it, simply by waking up and setting the reverse gear in motion . . . but it is no dream. This is real. This is the world, what is left of it, and like Hubbs and Kendra I must die out on the desert in an attempt to hold it together. I could do no less for them. I could do no less for humanity.

Do I romanticize? Sentimentalize? What has humanity ever done for me that I should be so sacrificing for humanity? But that is the problem, the heart of the nightmare . . . we are humanity and ask ourselves such questions. Self-interest versus altruism; preservation versus sacrifice.

The ants do not even consider it.

I am going to go out there. I do not feel very much like dying, particularly since these last few days with Kendra have, however terrible, given me an understanding of what life might be like. But it must be done. If I fail, and I do not see how I can succeed because there may be two queens out there under those mounds or thousands, I do not know what form the future may take . . . but I am sure that they have their plans.

I would really rather not think about their plans.

I am going to go out there now.

God help us all. But who is God?

XI

Lesko stumbled through the desert in an abscess of red and green, shrugging off the bites, which he could barely feel through the heavy metal gear. That had been Hubbs's mistake; he had been rubberized but Lesko was metallized. Metallic Lesko, clever, clever Lesko, he staggered through the desert for a hundred feet or a mile, it was all the same to him, and he came to the mounds and looked down upon them. And there in the slight crevice between them was a clear, black, hole pooled with liquid in which could only be the queen herself, and he raised the grenade—

—And the ground shifted beneath his feet.

—And Lesko fell into the opening.

It seemed to him incredible at first that he could fall because he was so much larger than this opening, surely it could not be more than a foot, a foot and a half across, but he entered very easily and then, slickly, he was sliding down. Green and gold on the sides, the fall effortless for all of its velocity, and Lesko did not feel fear so much as curiosity; where would he land? Into what rabbit hole had the ants plunged him? He landed on his feet with a small jolt before he could consider this further and found himself in an enclosure permeated by a hum; he turned then and saw the dead eyes of the queen. There was the queen. He had been falling toward her all the time. He lifted the grenade launcher and walked toward her. The queen hummed.

He lifted the launcher and the humming decreased in pitch. He could bring it down and smash the queen. She was a dead, brown husk with a thousand holes for eyes. He could break her like ash. He did not. He stood there.

Kendra came from somewhere.

She was dressed in flowing white, and her eyes were filled with love. She raised her hands to him, then her arms, and Lesko dropped the grenade launcher. It fell without sound. She came against him and he felt her body, inhaled the gentle scent that came from her. He stroked her hair. She huddled against him. Under the queen's eyes, he kissed her forehead. Kendra looked at him. She could see his suffering, he knew. She could tell what it had cost him to come. To merge with her. To be both more and less than himself. She pointed toward the queen.

"Do they want us?" he said.

She held her hand level and in her eyes he saw words. Then it was as if he could see into her mind, and there was no need at all for words. There was communication on a different level. He was no longer Lesko; she was no longer Kendra. She was Lendralesko; he was Leskokendra; they were one creature.

He moved toward the queen.

The queen received him, and he saw—

XII

The landscape: black trees with blue leaves against a yellow sky, the sky like a dome, plunging, billowing, becoming a red ocean, the foam yellow heaving on the violet rocks, the green sun splashing red spray in front of it; the birds, the dark birds, the purple birds, folding into the grayness and the rose, the bloody, full lips of the rose as it leaned forward to kiss the air as it came from a flower and then the landscape shifting, stripped, a bare tree like a face in the glow of something that was and was not the sun, rays protruding from that illumination like hands, the hands lifting—

—A huge granite rock suspending it over the floor that became an ocean, and the ocean flowing, flowing into a naked women, a kendraleskoleskokendra lying on a beach and from between her legs the sun bursting forth and the colony folded and flowing over them as—

X̄III

They mounted a hill in another place open against the sky. Lesko saw the sun and it was in her hair, shining like a firmament through Kendra's hair. The sun was inside her; she was the sun, his queen then, and he closed against her. Her voice was in his mind without words.

"We have a choice," she was saying. "They've given us a choice."

"Yes," he said, also without words, understanding then, feeling that he understood everything at last and was drawn unto the queen, his queen, fingers flowing, both of them flowing, and then they were wound and falling together—

X̄IV

Down a long tube that terminated in air, he and she fell through it together and—

XV

From that tube was an embryo, eyes growing, legs
bursting through, first fishlike, then birdlike, mamma-
lian, and then it was an ant and then it was not; instead it had become a human fetus, the fetus growing,
growing and filling the landscape until at last it
possessed it fully, no longer a fetus but a baby, a child,
clustering with animals: lions, birds, bears, huge
towers in the distance with indecipherable writing upon
it on which more animals gamboled, and the child
walked toward it slowly, carrying the sun in his hand,
the universe in a fold of its flesh, all of eternity in a
palm—

XVI

"What is this?" Hubbs said and came to light.

XVII

"We're saved," Eldridge said, and then he saw—

XVIII

"What has happened?" Mildred said and—

XIX

Clete was running, running desperately, screaming, but he could not get away and then—

XX

HUBBSELDRIDGEMILDREDCLETE: On a mountain somewhere folded together in the talons of a stone, gripped in a fist that was a heart—

XXI

LESKOKENDRA: Looked at the thing on the other side of the mountain. Between it and them were the heads of ants. Ants were perched on their little cilia, looking at them with understanding and compassion. Eyes blinked; the ants signaled and they signaled back. The crawling thing on the other side of the mountain labored toward them and then stopped as the ants stroked it.

The dead green and yellow light came from behind them as they held together on the mountain. It bathed them and they felt its warmth. It was all that they— and the thing on the other side—would ever need.

A voice said, "Clear all channels. Clear all channels. Please clear all channels," and phase five began.